TRACI JO STOTTS

Evernight Teen ®

www.evernightteen.com

Copyright© 2015

Traci Jo Stotts

ISBN: 978-1-77233-660-3

Cover Artist: Jay Aheer

Editor: JC Chute

TRACI JO STOTTS

DEDICATION

I have many people to thank. First, as always, thank you to my Heavenly Father, for blessing me with the ability to tell tales.

To my mom, thank you for choosing to listen to my stories over the car stereo on our road trips, I'll cherish those memories always. To my siblings—Debbie, Scott and Shannon, thank you for being my first best friends.

David, you hold the key to my heart. Thank you for supporting me and giving me everything I want. My boyz, Bubb, Zach and Mattman, being your mom is my greatest title.

Thank you, Kim, for answering all of my questions and giving guidance and support. To my beta readers, Tammy, Juanita and Sarah, thank you for giving my words your time.

To my two biggest fans. Spring, you cheered me on chapter after chapter, urging me to keep going. Without you, FROM SHATTERED PIECES might not have come to fruition. Kris, your words are what every writer wants to hear. You made me feel like a rock star and gave me the confidence to take the next step in this wild adventure.

Thank you.

TRACI JO STOTTS

FROM SHATTERED PIECES

Traci Jo Stotts

Copyright © 2015

Chapter One

I don't know why at this moment my brother, who died before I was even born, pops into my head. At first, the look on my father's face is one of sadness but it quickly turns to rage. I guess I've had all I could take from him. I meant what I said. Timmy was the lucky one.

I'm ready for him: his clenched fists with white knuckles. His poisonous words, mixed with spit, land on my skin and pierce my ears as I brace myself for the pain. I look around for my mother, who usually disappears during my father's fits of rage, and as I expect she is nowhere in sight. I don't need her. This has been my life for so long, it's all I know.

My father is not a big man, but he's strong. I'm very quick, and today I'm so filled with adrenaline, I feel like I can shoot through the ceiling, like a comic book superhero.

He swings his clenched fist at my face and I duck at the last second. He spins around and clumsily trips over the coffee table, sending its contents to the floor in a scattered mess. Before he has the chance to stand upright, my shoe meets the side of his head.

"Ian! What've you done?" Now my mother stands there holding her hands to her colorless face. It infuriates me that in all the years of beatings she has never once intervened. No hugs or caresses in the dark afterward, either. She would just carry on as if everything was normal. But nothing in my house has ever been normal.

At the sound of her voice, my father begins to stir a bit. I kick him again before my mother can take another step closer to us. I look down, first at the crumpled mess of a man on the floor, then at my mother. I move so close to my mother our noses are touching. "Don't you dare come looking for me! If anyone asks, you tell them I went to live with an aunt in Tennessee or an uncle in Florida. You make up any story you want!" Both my mother and I know these relatives don't exist, but she'll need to have a story ready if anyone asks.

Pushing by her, I rush down the hall to my room, tossing my backpack onto my bed and filling it with only my most treasured belongings. I make sure to pack my toothbrush, my Ozzy hoodie, some clean panties, and flip-flops, along with a change of clothes. I'm almost back into the living room, where my mother is sure to be helping my father, when I spot the file cabinet in the corner of the den. I'm on my knees pulling folders out until I find what I'm looking for, shoving my birth certificate and Social Security card into my pack. Before leaving the den, I empty my father's coffee can into my outside pocket. This is where they keep their beer money. They'll miss the money a lot more than they'll miss me. No doubt about that.

I make my way to the kitchen and am shocked to see my mother sitting at the table, not kneeling next to my father trying to nurse him back to life. Her hands are still cupped to her face. I'm not about to have a mother-daughter moment now, so I reach behind her for a jar of peanut butter and a sleeve of crackers.

"I'm sorry." Her words are barely a whisper.

"What?" Surely, I misunderstood her. Still, my breath catches in my throat and my limbs stiffen.

"I'm sorry you were ever born." Her hands, now folded on the table in front of her.

Now that's more like it. My mother, the one human being on the planet who is supposed to love me unconditionally and protect me from all evil, almost has me believing she cares. Almost.

I slam the back door with every bit of strength I can muster and am pleased to hear the panels of glass shatter, littering the ground and floor. With shaky fingers, I unlatch the gate and turn for one last glance at the life I'm leaving behind forever. Nope, can't say I'll miss it. The gate closes behind me and I begin walking towards the bright city lights of Reno.

The full moon dims with each step closer to the casino and its flashing neon lights, until it disappears altogether behind the tall hotel towers. I weave in and out of the casinos, as I've done a million times. When my parents would get their drink on, I'd climb out my bedroom window and walk around until I knew they'd be passed out.

Families walk by laughing and pointing at the games on the midway or visit as they wait in line for the buffet. Sometimes I linger to take in the kind words spoken between them.

I make my way to the ladies' room and plop down into an ugly paisley chair surrounded by gaudy gold-trimmed mirrors. I count out how much money my parents gave me. Yes, that sounds better than how much money I stole. Sixty-three dollars. I stuff the money into my shoe and wonder if it'll be enough to get me to California.

Not sure what my next move is, I curl my legs under me and recall the events of the day. I woke up early, before my alarm, as I do every morning. I ate some leftover stuffing for breakfast, passed my chemistry quiz, and completed all of my chores before my father got home. Well, *almost* all of my chores. It was an honest mistake. I'd only forgotten the trashcan that sits next to his chair once before. He told me he was going to make sure I'd never forget again. I guess he was wrong.

A spanking was never just a spanking in the Ross household. I don't know what I did to my father to make him hate me so. He didn't save all of his rage for me— no, my mother also had her share. That's why it's so sickening she could sit by, when she knows perfectly well what a punch from him feels like.

I was used to his "punishments": slaps and kicks or being pulled this way or that, usually by my hair. But today he said one too many hateful things to me and I couldn't keep my angry thoughts to myself any longer. I don't recall the exact words I used, but I know I told him to go fuck himself a time or two.

A glance into the mirror reveals a black eye and I can still taste the blood from the cut on my lip. "What an asshole."

I have a year-and-a-half until I turn eighteen, and then I will be free. I'm out of the house and away from them … but for how long? They can find me and make me go back. That is not an option. I really don't expect them to come find me. I just have to figure out a way to take care of myself until I'm considered legal. Taking care of myself I'm used to, but that was in my parents' house. Out here, I am totally alone.

Before sheer panic can take over, I'm up and wandering the casino. My mind is racing in a million different directions. I sit at the counter in the diner and scribble on the back of a Keno ticket.

Find a place to live.

Maybe if I start smaller, this won't be so difficult.

Find a place to sleep tonight.

I stare at the paper and remember the river. Lots of people sleep along the riverbanks. My lips relax into a half-smile when a very old waitress with very tall hair and way too much makeup slaps a menu down and asks me what I want to drink. "I'll have a root beer."

Three refills later, I pay my tab and get my nerve up to make the trek to the river, checking to make sure I'm carrying a pocket-knife. Tim Walters gave it to me in the sixth grade for letting him feel me up behind the gym. I love that memory now—so silly, and so innocent.

My life hasn't always been so dark and sad. I had lots of friends and school was always a place where I felt comfortable. The teachers liked me and I liked them. They told me I was smart and praised me when I did a good job. I soaked that up like a sponge. It wasn't only the teachers who made me love school, though—it was football. A group of boys played, every recess and lunch break. It just so happens I was better than most of them. My girlfriends would cheer me on and we'd rub it into the boys' faces that they were just outplayed by a girl.

Home was always a lonely place. But it wasn't always so angry. I think I was six when my dad first hit me—before then, he had only hit my mother. I was trying to get help with my homework. I lost my balance and fell onto his lap, leaving a long trail of black marker up his pant leg. I had to stay home for a couple of days because the bruise on my cheek was too dark to hide behind my mother's makeup. My friends began to pull away from me in junior high school … or me from them. Either way,

11

I no longer had a group of friends laughing and cheering me on. I still did everything I could to impress my teachers. I needed the validation.

I step out into the warm night air, still lost in my thoughts. The streets are abuzz with people, mostly tourists. A group of guys stumble past me, whooping it up about the strippers and how someone named *Mark* still has a hard-on. I have to step out into the street to get around another group. This group is not young guys, but a bunch of senior citizens in town for a poker tournament. Some have walkers and a couple of them have power scooters, which is the reason I have to step out into the street. It's that, or I get run over by *Mable* and her motorized death mobile.

The closer I get to the river, the emptier the streets get. I've never been this far from South Virginia Street. The buzzing lights are far behind me now and I find myself regretting my bright idea to stay the night at the river. I doubt I'll get any sleep. Maybe home isn't so bad. Who am I kidding? I can never go back. He'll kill me for sure.

My mind wanders to my parents. I try to stop myself from wondering what I did wrong. I washed dishes, vacuumed, and even cleaned toilets, and they never had to ask for a cold beer. I was trained that way, from the time I could open the fridge by myself.

A woman's scream brings me back to the present, and I stop just in time to avoid getting smacked by a door being flung open and two drunken idiots being hauled out by the largest black man I've ever seen. He simply carries them by the napes of their necks like they're dolls. The woman adjusts her too-high heels, and waves her long fake fingernails in his face.

"Let go of him, you asshole. He didn't even do

anything. It was that prick who started it." She reaches out to scratch an already bleeding man, but he tilts his head back and manages to push her away with his dangling leg.

I am frozen to the spot. This is the coolest thing I've ever seen. The lady reminds me of a chubby Dolly Parton impersonator. She is total white trash and owning it in every possible way, but her man looks like my chemistry teacher: tall and skinny, with glasses riding the tip of his nose.

The enormous black man doesn't care to hear the debate. "I'll let you go if you agree to shut up and go your separate ways. Got it?"

"I got it," Dolly's man says. His pale skin has turned red and purple from lack of oxygen. "Shhhh!" he shouts, as Dolly opens her mouth to protest.

"I'm not screwin' wit'cha. I'll put a boot in your asses if you continue this bullshit." Jubal releases them. "Go on, now. I don't get paid to babysit."

The three keep their promise and head in separate directions. Only when the couple is about to turn the corner does "Dolly" turn around and scream some profanity with both middle fingers held high in the other guy's direction.

I'm still standing there like a moron when he notices me. "What the hell? Out a bit late, ain't ya?" He's grinning the smallest grin.

"What are you, my babysitter?" I return his grin but inside I'm scared and my legs are shaking so bad he's sure to notice. I adjust my backpack and sidestep around him.

"Better sleep with one eye open, crazy white girl." He sees my expression change from a fake grin to a look of pure disbelief. "Don't gimme that look. Where're you headin?" He gives a chuckle that irritates me. I'm about to tell him so, when the door flings open and an older woman who has spent more time in the sun than out of it hollers at him.

"Jubal, get your big black ass in here and take care of this!" she demands, as she flicks her cigarette butt into the gutter.

"The freaks come out at night. Huh, Sylvia?" Jubal adjusts his shirt.

"Apparently." Sylvia disappears inside.

I'm happy for the interruption, because Jubal's talking like he's inside my head and I don't like it. I'm no more than a few steps away when he calls out, "You take care, and I'm not kiddin' when I tell ya sleep with one eye open. Crazy white girl." He's gone when I turn to ask him if he has a better idea of where I'm supposed to sleep.

I get to the river and wonder if I'll ever sleep at all. The people around me are twitchy and dirty, and their eyes look too big for their sockets. There are groups of people standing around garbage can fires, couples sharing sleeping bags, and one guy barking at a tree. I stay far away from all of them as I continue looking for a place to hide away. There's a chain-link fence with large bushes growing along it, and upon closer inspection I see a hollow. I crawl inside and look for any signs this spot belongs to anyone. I find nothing. I'm hard to see, if I can be seen at all, which helps slow my pulse a bit. I'm freaking out because of Jubal's stupid words of wisdom.

I count out what's left of my money after root beer and a burrito from the gas station, then stuff the folded cash into my shoe. I put my Ozzy Osbourne hoodie on over the backpack and curl up in the fetal position. It's the most comfortable I can get and I really feel like a helpless infant.

"What am I doing here?" I ask the dark sky above me.

I spend an eternity sorting through memories, making plans for my future, thinking my first stop in the morning will be the bus station. I'll buy a ticket to anywhere in California and bum around trying to find work until I'm able to sign myself back into school and get my diploma. Until then, I have no parental permission to do anything. I don't want to, but I find myself thinking about my mother and father and I have to remind myself that yes, they are *that* bad. Sometimes our minds can trick us into thinking situations aren't as bad as we believe. It's a tool of survival: you can continue with the familiar, if you make yourself believe you're happy.

I feel something crawl across my leg. I don't care what it is—I just brush it away as quietly as possible. There's a flashlight on a keychain, but I'm afraid to turn it on. The slightest noise or movement of a branch causes me to jump. I want to run back to the bar and tell Jubal to get his big black ass down here and make these people stay far away from me. I also have my Walkman, but I'm afraid to take away my sense of hearing. I fall asleep with a death grip on my pocketknife.

～～～～～～

The birds wake me with their morning chatter. I sit straight up and let out a scream. All of a sudden I don't care who knows where I'm hiding. "Assholes!"

I'm trying hard to figure out how this happened. I was worried I wouldn't be able to sleep and it turns out I was in a coma. My bare feet are freezing. I pull off my hoodie and inspect my backpack. I'm relieved they only needed my shoes—my shoes, and every penny I had to my name. "Shit!" I put on my flip-flops and start running. I run by Sylvia's, which makes me want to scream, and I keep running.

Suddenly my chest is aching from the realization of having nowhere to go and nobody to help me. Thinking of my brother almost forces me to my knees. Since the night I heard my parents fighting about him I've held onto the memory of a big brother who, if still alive, would protect me and love me. I know it's impossible, but I can see his face. I hear his laughter. I hear him say my name. I love my brother. The irony is if my brother were still alive I would never have been born. I learned that same night they only had me to replace their beloved departed son.

My father blamed my mother and she blamed him. He called one afternoon when she was out in the yard with Timmy. She knew what would happen to her if she missed his call, so without thinking she ran inside. The sound of the braking vehicle caused her to drop the phone and rush back outside, but it was too late. Timmy's white ball with the blue stripe and red star on each side rolled into the gutter. There was nothing anyone could do.

They thought if they had another son to cherish, they might be happy again.

Leaning against a tree, I push the memories from my head. They're a waste of time and I can't deal with that. I have enough stress with the here and now. I walk into a casino and head straight to the restroom. What a mess. The girl in the mirror has leaves in her tangled hair and dirt smudged on her cheek. I change into clean clothes and work my long messy hair into anything not resembling a rat's nest.

I go to Rosie's Café and ask for a booth for three. "My parents are on their way down." This is a simple and believable lie. While in the booth I sip ice water, and keep looking around for my parents to show. I open a jelly packet and stick my pinky in the sweet gooeyness when the waitress insists I order. Hunger beats out the fact I have no money, so I order the breakfast special: ham steak with eggs over-medium, hash browns, and sourdough toast for $2.99.

I sit here thinking about fourth period Foods class, when John and Travis told the whole class how they went to Suzie's Steakhouse and ordered huge porterhouse steak dinners and then rushed out without paying. The waitress found them outside standing by their truck arguing over who was going back inside for the keys. She just laughed as she twirled the keys on her porky finger. Travis' dad was a lawyer who spoiled him so he enjoyed the story immensely. John, however, was not as lucky. His mother was so upset he'd taken advantage of working people she made him go back to Suzie's and wash dishes for eight hours, two Saturdays in a row.

As I sit here licking every speck of food off my enormous plate, I am consumed with guilt. I can't do this. I might vomit. I'm not sure if it's the actual guilt or the horrendous amount of food I just shoveled into my body. My waitress mistakes the tears in my eyes for sadness because my parents have yet to arrive. She tells me not to worry about the three-dollar ticket. "Go on upstairs and get your parents. I'll be here and I'm not worried about it." She gives my shoulder a light pat with her bony arthritic fingers.

I move slowly through the casino. The binging and dinging sounds of the machines are temporarily blocking any thoughts from forming in my mind. I get to the door and feel a hand on my shoulder. It is not the bony-handed waitress. *Oh, shit. Security.* I freeze, but do not turn.

"You're not really going to leave without your parents, are you?"

"Jubal?" I look up to see him smiling from ear to ear and chuckling. "Shut up! You have no idea how bad I feel right now." I hit him, but am positive it hurts my hand more than his solid arm.

"Come with me." Jubal waves one of his enormous hands.

I take two steps with him before stopping fast. "Gimme five bucks." I hold out my hand. "Come on!"

He slaps a five-dollar bill in my hand and watches me speed-walk back into the diner. I return with the biggest smile, and at that moment I feel happy.

Chapter Two

Jubal leads me to a motorcycle in the parking garage. He tosses me a helmet and points to the back of his bike. I've never even sat on a motorcycle before. My body is shaking so badly I think I might fall off, and I'm hoping against hope Jubal can't tell how nervous I am. I don't even care where he's taking me, just as long as I get away from the cokeheads who took my shoes and money—and even farther away from my parents.

The feeling of the wind swirling all around me as Jubal speeds down the freeway is so exhilarating. I've never felt such excitement. He might be trying to scare me, because he's weaving in and out of vehicles like you'd see in a chase scene of a movie. I lean my head back, close my eyes and laugh. I laugh so hard Jubal yells at me asking if I'm okay. He must think I'm scared.

Jubal steers the bike off of the interstate and onto CA-20 W. We're in California. I guess I didn't need the sixty dollars after all. Stupid druggies. I'm taking in the warmth of the sunshine when Jubal brings the bike to a stop. I grab tightly to his middle for the first time, looking around for a reason why we've stopped in the middle of nowhere. He parks his bike under a huge shade tree that holds at least a million shoes, of all styles and sizes. I stare into it trying to count them, but I'm interrupted by Jubal, hopping off the bike and pulling off his helmet. He turns on me, his face flooded with anger.

I look in both directions trying to find the source of his rage, but we are the only two people on this long stretch of highway. He's gripping his helmet like a melon he wants to crush.

"What the hell is wrong with you? Just leave with a man who you don't even know. I could be John-frickin'-Gacy for all you know. Get on a man's bike and let him take you anywhere. Really?" Jubal is now yelling his rant.

I can see he is genuinely pissed. I try to explain before the bulging veins in his neck explode. "First, I do know you. You're Jubal. Second, I'm pretty sure John Wayne Gacy preferred boys… and third, my gut tells me you'd never hurt little ol' me!" I bat my eyelashes and give my most adorable grin.

The veins begin to flatten and his jaw muscles relax. A roar from deep in his belly explodes and he fills my ears with a high-pitched laugh, sending me rolling off his bike.

"Crazy… white… girl!" This is all he can manage in between fits of laughter.

Once we are both capable of breathing again, we climb back onto the bike and he asks me my name.

"Ian. Ian Ross." I wait for the reaction I always get, but he's too worn out from laughing so he just manages to glance at me with his friendly smile. "No shit?"

Back on the road we begin to climb in elevation and the earth drops off freakishly close to the narrow highway. The trees are thick, and Jubal points out several waterfalls peeking through the green. He maneuvers the bike around the hairpin curves with ease.

We reach a town called Cavern Creek. It's a small town with a handful of shops on the main street. Jubal pulls into the parking lot of a diner. He must've heard my tummy grumbling. I'm small, but I have a huge appetite. Learning to cook when I was seven has been helpful. I remind him I have absolutely no cash.

"That's okay, Ian. They'll let you wash dishes," Jubal teases.

We sit in a booth and he asks me several

questions. Why did I run? Who gave me the black eye? General questions about my messed-up life. He also shares a little about himself. He told me he ran away once. He grew up in foster homes until he was adopted in his early teens.

"So, is that where we're heading? To meet your brother Jim?" It takes a lot of self-control to not ask the million questions I have in my head at this moment.

"No. I'm taking you to my place. It's complicated. I still don't know if my plan is a good one or completely stupid. You will have to do things you might not be comfortable doing." He pauses to take a drink of his sweet tea, and to see my reaction.

"You're a pimp? I'm still a virgin! You asshole. Man, was my gut wrong about you!" I grab my backpack and am about to scoot out of the booth when Jubal lets out his high-pitched laugh. I can't help but join him. "Please don't be a pimp."

"Girl, you crazy! I will tell you what I am and what I do, but not here, so finish your lunch." He wipes the tears from his cheeks and eats the last of his chili fries.

Jubal drives ten minutes out of town. When he turns off the main road I'm reminded of a painting I saw in a museum on a field trip I took in the third grade. The road was grassy with two lines of dirt where tires had formed a path. There were tall shade trees on both sides and the sunlight danced through the leaves above.

We pull up to a large ranch house. It's a pale yellow with an enormous porch wrapping around the entire place. There is a window on the second floor that is boarded up. There are several missing shutters. It's in need of serious TLC. Jubal drives around to the side and parks inside a large garage with several vehicles in different stages of repair.

"So, you're not a pimp. You run a chop shop?" I pull my helmet off and am shocked when a guy with bright red hair takes it from me. He's short but very muscular, with a lot of tattoos. Most of them are naked ladies. Very classy. I don't like him, not because of the tattoos but the way he looks at me. It's like he wants to punch me. I know that look.

"Jubal, where've you been, man? We were supposed to leave an hour ago." The man looks at me sideways, and then back to Jubal, eyebrows raised. Subtle.

"Take it easy. Let me show Ian here inside and we'll go. You always make us leave too early anyway, and we end up having to wait forever. This is Ian, by the way. Ian, Mikus." Neither of us offers a hand or even a nod.

The inside of the house is even larger than it looks from the outside. Jubal leads me through the messy kitchen and down a hallway. There's another, separate hallway in the back of the house also. Jubal tells me to avoid that part of the house. "I gotta go for a few hours. Make yourself at home and we'll talk when I get back. You'll be safe. You can hang out in my room and watch TV."

I can't help feeling like a dumb sixteen-year-old. I leave the state with the first male who shows me kindness. Serious daddy issues. "Really gotta be gone for hours? Does anyone else live here?"

"No. It's just me and Mikus. I really gotta go before he gets any more pissed off. Irish tempers, you know?" Jubal pulls the door shut behind him and hollers something to Mikus I can't make out. They leave in a Blazer rather than on their bikes. I wonder if Mikus has one. I'm too scared to go outside so I make a mental note to wander when Jubal gets back.

I lock the deadbolt on his door, climb into the softest recliner ever made, and click on the television. *Knight Rider* it is. I pull the handle on the side of the chair, kicking out the leg rest with my feet, and cuddle up with a blanket.

Next thing I know, I'm being awakened by Jubal. The sky outside is dark. I must've fallen asleep. I rub my eyes and stretch, noticing his dark mood.

Jubal paces the floor in front of me a couple of times. I ask him to stop making me dizzy and sit down. He tells me a little about his past and how he ended up here. I learn this ranch belongs to Mikus. Jubal worked for Mikus in his garage in town, until he lost it when he got back into drugs. Nobody else would even give Jubal an interview when he got out of jail. After the shop closed, he continued fixing cars here at the ranch and went back to selling drugs. Now he's only doing it until he has enough money put away to open up a garage of his own in Mission Valley.

"You're a drug dealer?" I'm in full yawn so I'm not sure he can make out my words.

"My point is, I want to help you, but you have to know the whole truth. I'm not a bad guy but I'm not that good either. You can stay here, or you can tell me *no* and I'll take you right back to Reno." Jubal stands up to pace again. He twists his hands trying to find the words he's searching for.

"Jubal. I don't know all you went through in your childhood, but I cannot go back to my parents. I can keep the house clean and I know how to cook. You can teach me how to work on cars and how to ride a motorcycle." I grin up at him.

23

"You can stay in the room across the hall. You take care of the house for your room and board. We don't have a lot of people over here. We used to have a house full of strange people all the time, but we had to put a stop to that when our stuff kept coming up missing."

"Jubal, can I just move a mattress in here? I won't be in your way." The thought of being in my own room without Jubal there to protect me from Mikus gives me the chills.

"You don't need to be sharing a room with a grown-ass man. If you'll feel better, I'll put a deadbolt on for you."

Jubal goes on to tell me Mikus has been really stressed lately, so I need to stay out of his way. I don't like Mikus anyway. His beady eyes scare me.

I'm not sure why I want to stay with Jubal but I can't imagine leaving. I know I can't go home. My father would chain me to the house like a dog. Jubal makes me laugh and I feel safe with him. I don't even mind the drugs. My mother has been hooked on Valium for as long as I can remember. Jubal lets me sleep in the recliner for the night, or what's left of it.

I sleep most of the morning away, but I manage to get breakfast and coffee made before the guys stumble into the kitchen. After we eat I ask Jubal if I can look around the place. The ranch house is big and from what I can see out of the window the land it sits on seems to go on forever. After walking around a bit I find Jubal in the garage working on an old pickup. He asks me to hand him a wrench and to his surprise, I know my way around a toolbox.

It's a nice day, mostly due to Mikus having left right after he drank most of the coffee and ate a few bites of the scrambled eggs I made. He mumbled something to Jubal about making a run to Reno and headed out. He'll be gone for probably a week.

~~~~~~~~~~~~~~~~~

Mikus pulls up but doesn't come in right away. He paces the driveway a few times before slamming the screen door to the kitchen. It smells delicious but Mikus looks unimpressed. I notice my hands begin to shake so I close my eyes and steady myself. "I'm making stroganoff. Are you hungry?" I try to sound cheerful, but inside I'm disappointed the week is up already.

"Jubal, what the hell is she still doing here? I told you, we ain't babysitters. We have grown up things goin' on here." He doesn't even acknowledge my question. Jerk.

"I'm not a baby. I know about your big boy business." Right as the words are out of my mouth I regret them. Jubal looks at me with disappointment.

"Shit, Jubal!" Mikus grabs a beer from the fridge and leans on the counter.

"Man, she has nowhere to go. She's harmless. Besides, I'm tired of eating your nasty cookin'. I told her she can stay in the room across the hall from mine," Jubal explains.

Mikus chugs his beer and sits across from Jubal in silence for a few minutes. I turn the burner off and dish up three plates of stroganoff with green beans. I pour milk for each of us and serve buttered bread. Halfway through his plate Mikus stops eating and has a huge creepy grin across his face. "I've got an idea. How 'bout the little girl starts a delivery business?"

"Absolutely not, man. I didn't save her from a life on the street to bring her into a life of drug dealin'."

I'm staring at my plate, afraid to swallow the food in my mouth. I know if I clear my mouth I will say something stupid. I can already see the anger in Jubal's eyes if the thought in my head escapes my lips.

"I'll do it." I don't even swallow, my mouth still full of food, before I mumble the words.

Jubal punches his fists down on the table. Both Mikus and I jump. I notice the beady-ness in Mikus' eyes fades to a pathetic haze of fear when Jubal gets angry. I like it.

"Mikus, come with me. Ian, get this food put away and clean up."

I nod in reply.

Jubal comes inside just as I am finishing up the dishes. I can tell he's mad at me. I don't even know what to say to him. I decide to keep quiet.

"Did you get the blankets washed?"

"Yes."

"Get your bed made up and get some sleep. We'll be leaving early." Jubal looks and sounds exhausted.

"Are you taking me back to Reno? I can't go back, Jubal. I won't go back!" I plead with him.

"Just get some sleep. I have some work to do tomorrow and I'm taking you with me." Jubal is holding his hand up to end the conversation, but I can't stand for him to be so upset with me.

"Okay, but I'm driving my own motorcycle." My hands are firmly on my hips.

This brings a small chuckle from Jubal. Not the belly laugh I was hoping for, but I'll take it. I go to my room, make my bed, and push the dresser in front of the door. I heard Mikus drive off earlier but he'll be back. Since the moment I met him, being in his presence feels like actual hands around my throat—like he's killing me.

Chapter Three

Jubal wasn't kidding. It feels like I barely close my eyes at all before he knocks on my door. I hear him laugh when I push the dresser back to its original spot.

"Here, I made us coffee." Jubal hands me a coffee mug from *Topless Todd's*. "It's almost a three-hour trip. Don't forget your bag... Oh, and we'll pick up a lock while we're out so you can stop rearranging furniture."

"Ha, ha. Thanks for the coffee. Where are we going?" I adjust the strap of my backpack and sip the coffee. I almost gag.

"I told you. I got some business to take care of. Just enjoy the ride."

Jubal leads me out to the garage. I'm happy to see him throw his bags into the back of the black and silver Blazer. I'm so tired I don't think I can balance on the back of a motorcycle for ten minutes, let alone three hours. The coffee tastes like battery acid. My eyes feel weighted. This is going to be a long trip.

"There's a blanket in the back. You can crash if you want." Jubal nods his head to the rear seat.

I climb over the seat and reach for the blanket. My short arms can't quite reach it. For some reason, Jubal enjoys this immensely. "You think this is funny? Not all of us were born jolly and green."

"Oh, it's like *that*? Your attitude is bigger than you are! Believe that."

I manage to grab the blanket, pleased to find it's one of the blankets I've just washed. I buckle into the front seat and ball up my hoodie into a pillow. I twist my hair between my fingers and force down the coffee.

As we drive through the main street of Cavern Creek, I notice how old it looks. Not much improvement or remodeling happens here. It's a small town. Jubal points out the different businesses and names of the people he knows. "Stay away from the Johnson boys, no matter how cute you think they are." Jubal points to three freckly redheads walking on the sidewalk.

"Shut up! I'm not into boys. I mean, I haven't even had a boyfriend yet." My eyes roll at the absurdity of his demand.

Jubal laughs out loud at my blushing cheeks. I, however, do not enjoy this feeling.

The coffee must kick in, because I am suddenly wide-awake. "Hey. Let's play a game."

"I *thought* you were goin' to sleep."

"I did too. Come on, let's play. We take turns asking questions. If the question is too hard to answer we can have one pass each. You down?" I pull my legs up to sit cross-legged, and then turn my body towards Jubal.

"Okay. Why are you so short?" Jubal cracks up laughing.

"Jubal!" I try to be mad but it's useless. I'm lost in laughter.

"Okay. Okay. First question. How'd you get the busted-up face?"

Most of the bruising has faded but the cut on my lip is taking its sweet time healing. I take a deep breath and tell him—in great detail—about the night I left my parents' house. He squeezes the steering wheel when I describe the hits and kicks my father got in before I finally stood up for myself. At that part of the story, Jubal's eyes light up. Throughout my explanation, he cheers me on. He doesn't interrupt me, he just kind of whispers things like, *go on* and *you tell 'em*. It feels good to finally tell somebody and stop using the, "I fell down the stairs" line.

"My turn, now. So how'd you end up with Mikus?"

"Well, to answer that I'd have to answer a lot of other questions. I met him in jail. He was spoiled and dumb. He was in for his second DUI and drug charges. I was waiting on my trial for robbery and assault. I saved his ass in the yard. He helped me when I got out."

"Did you do it?"

"I did. I was eighteen and hung with a gang. I was told to go to the Food Mart and rob this Chinese guy, the owner. I get all pumped up, right? Thinking I'm the man. I go in and get him nice and scared. He was really bad with English and the more upset he got, the harder it was to understand him. I demand the cash from the register. He's mumbling and nodding his head. My adrenaline is pumped up and I want more. I tell him to take me to the safe. He tells me there is no safe, so I fake like I'm gonna hit him. He stumbles to the office in the rear of the store. When he gets to the door, he pauses. He says, "Please don't", so I give him a nudge. The door opens and his pregnant wife is sitting at the desk filling out an order or something."

"No way." I'm glued to his every word.

"Yea. She has this tape player in there, playing lullabies. American lullabies. Anyway, we startle her and her smile turns to fear when she sees her husband. He tells her something in Chinese. She just nods at me. I remember how she nodded, rubbed her belly and kept singing, real quiet-like."

"You couldn't go through with it, huh?"

"No. But I couldn't go back to my guys without the money. So I just say I'm sorry, but I gotta do what I was told. They both just nodded and continued to get into the safe. I made him stop. I told the lady to call the police. I placed the money on the desk and just repeated, "I'm sorry". Then I pull my hood off and walk slowly to the door. I knew my crew would be watchin' so I wait until I saw lights and walk out the door. Didn't even make it out of the parking lot."

"Oh my gosh. So, if you put the money on the desk, how'd you get robbery and assault?"

Jubal looked at me with his kind grin. "You quick, girl."

"Can you pull over soon? I have to pee after drinking all that nasty coffee."

"Ouch. You baggin' on my coffee? I see. I see. There's a rest area in about ten miles. Can you wait that long?" Jubal teases.

"Sure. Back to your story."

"Well, the cops pull up with guns pulled, sirens, lights. Get me on the pavement quick. Throw my ass in jail for eighteen months. When the case finally went to trial, I was scared to death they was gonna hang me until Mrs. Lee sat in the witness stand. I just took a deep breath. She looked at me and nodded. She had the same effect on me as she did that night in the store. She saved my ass. She told them there was no money missing and nobody was hurt. I still got five years."

"So, you met up with Mikus when you got out?"

"Exactly. We're here."

"What'd you do with the gun?" My eyes are on him and not our new surroundings.

"What gun? Do I look like I need a gun?" He laughs with flexed arms.

Jubal parks and I run to the restroom. We walk around a few minutes and stretch before getting back on the road. When we do, Jubal is right back to our game.

"What's up with your name?"

"You're asking *me* about *my* name? That's funny."

"Ouch!" Jubal laughs.

"My full name is Vivian. I think it's after my grandmother. I was supposed to be a boy. They never used my name. My mother always made me keep my hair long, which was weird because I thought they'd prefer a short boyish cut. But then I realized one morning, when I was getting ready for school... long hair hides the bruises. Anyways, tell me about your name. Is it your real name or a nickname?"

"It's my given name. Right on my birth certificate." Jubal holds his right hand up as if he's taking an oath.

"Well, I like it." I stare out the window. The scenery looks like Nevada, with lots of sagebrush and hills. After a while I notice weird trees popping up in the middle of the desert. They look like an alien cactus mixed with a palm tree. "What are those?"

"Those are chachi trees. They're really Joshua trees but I've always called 'em chachi trees. I like 'em. It's like they don't fit in anywhere so they have to survive together in the desert."

I look at Jubal and I think he's just as tired of our game as I am. I reach for the radio knob and it's tuned to country music—real *tears-in-my-beer* kind of stuff. We sit quietly for a while until I can no longer stand the sad country songs.

"Tell me more about Mikus."

"He really freaks you out, don't he?" I shrug for a reply and he continues. "He's an only child. His dad was very rich. He was also very mean. Mikus spent most of his time with his grandma. His parents gave up on him when they caught him with drugs in the house after his fourth time in jail. His grandma didn't agree with their approach. She continued to give him everything he asked for. The ranch house, she gave it to him. Just gave it to him. He kept it up until she passed. After that, it went to hell."

The scenery is changing into long stretches of forest. The desert land is transformed into thick walls of green. The windy roads take us up high into the mountains. The road signs warn of bear crossings. I stare out the window trying to focus on the blurred trees and rocks, hoping to see a bear.

"I'm hungry. I *know* you hungry. You always hungry." Jubal laughs as he shakes my shoulder. He's right—I'm starving.

"What? No restaurant?" I look at Jubal and back at the grocery store he's just pulled into.

"Nope. We show up at Jim's with a full belly, he'll grind us up and feed us to the pigs. We're gonna run in here and grab some greens and a bag of pork rinds."

It feels great to get out of the Blazer. It's chilly, so I pull my hoodie over my head and throw my messy hair into an enormous bun. My legs are numb and my back is killing me. We walk into the store and every bag of chips, every box of pasta, and even the cans of chili are making my mouth water.

"Is Jim nice or his he like *Mukus*?" I ask, hoping it's not the latter.

Jubal looks at me and I know it's a face telling me not to call him that to his face. "My brother is nothing like Mikus." He grins. "Mukus…!" he whispers as he drives out of the parking lot.

"Oh, cool. So, this is Mission Valley? It's pretty. The pine trees are enormous. I like how all the stores have a log cabin look. I can see why you want your garage here. Hey, can we go see it?" I ask, with genuine enthusiasm.

"Sure, It's on the way to Jim's. It's not nice like all of these shops you're lookin' at. But, it will be."

The sidewalks are full of people walking in and out of the shops. The tall mountains peak over the line of stores. "Hey, what are those?" I point to a long row of boxes on cables.

"Those are the gondolas that take you to the top of the mountain. You've never been skiing before? You've never been out of Reno, have you?"

"No, but you can take me!"

"You'll have to wait until mid-November. We have one more stop." Jubal pulls into the parking lot of Bubb's Fencing and Feed Store. "Can't show up without treats."

"Hey, Jubal! It's been a while! On your way to see Jim?" I see a young guy shaking Jubal's hand and without realizing it, I'm leaning into the side mirror to get a glimpse of myself. I'm pulling at the stray hairs that have escaped the wretched bun on the top of my head. I wipe the sleep from my eyes and rub the sleeve of my hoodie over my teeth.

"This, here, is Ian." He catches me in the mirror and a smile creeps onto his lips. I'm nauseated.

"Hi. I'm Sawyer." I shake his hand and instantly look down at the ground. I notice my feet, still in flip-flops. I suddenly wish for death.

"Are you here for the usual pick-up?" Sawyer smiles at me and turns to Jubal.

We load the feed into the Blazer and are on our way. I pray for a silent trip but I know Jubal can't wait to tease me. I'm right. As soon as we are out of the parking lot Jubal is laughing and talking in a high-pitched girly voice. I guess he's trying to sound like me. "My name is Ian. I'm not even into boys. I've never had a boyfriend."

"Shut up! I swear, Jubal, I've never acted like that before. I hope I never see him again. I'm totally embarrassed. The assholes at the river stole my shoes. I'm wearing the same pair of pants every day. I bet he thought I was homeless. Kill me now." I free my wild hair from the bun and hide my face. Jubal must see just how mortified I am, because he doesn't say another word about it.

"Look over there." Jubal points over my shoulder. What I see takes my breath away.

"Oh, Jubal. It's beautiful. It's so blue. What is that? Can we stop?"

"That is Indigo Lake. And, no, we need to get to Jim's."

I keep my eyes locked on the water until it no longer peeks through the breaks in the trees. When I look back at Jubal, he is smiling at me.

"The garage is right there." Jubal points with excitement and pride. All I see is a worn-down old garage that is probably condemned, but I hide my opinion behind a huge smile.

"Jubal, that's a great place! I can picture all the vehicles lined up waiting for you to work your magic." I really do believe he'll be great.

Jubal spends the rest of the twenty-minute drive to Jim's telling me his plans. He talks about how he's going to paint it, what the sign will look like, and how everyone will know where to go for honest and solid work. I love the sparkle in his eyes when he talks about things that are important to him. The big black scary guy with tattoos and scars fades, and all I see is the kindest person I've ever known.

We drive through a gate with a huge sign overhead made out of enormous pine posts and metal, reading "Freedom Farms". Jubal must see the awe in my gaze because he tells me how Jim designed and made the sign himself.

"He's an artist." Jubal beams with pride.

Jim's farm puts Mikus' ranch house to shame. The front of the log-style house has several windows. The house is skirted in a covered porch. A beautiful golden retriever dog sits on the top step, its tail wagging. "That's Fancy," Jubal tells me as he hands me the bag of pork rinds. "These are for her."

Jubal parks on the side of the house. I can see a barn and at least five different animals, not counting Fancy. This place is unbelievable. The woodwork is both solid and delicate. The fencing is made of brawny wood posts with three strands of barbed wire tying them together. I hop out of the Blazer and pet the llama standing close to the fence.

"Don't touch that nasty thing. Come on, let's go inside." Jubal guides me to the house with his nose wrinkled in disgust, all the while looking cautiously at the llama.

"Are you afraid of llamas?" I start to tease him when a deep voice interrupts me.

"That's not a llama, it's an alpaca. And he's still mad at her for the sour mouth." I turn expecting to see another black giant, but see a man that could've just walked out of a John Wayne movie. Jim is a tall, muscular, jeans-clad, cowboy-hat-wearing white man.

Chapter Four

"Hey, brother. Man, it's good to see you." Jim walks down the porch steps, wraps his arms around Jubal and pats him hard on the back. "Who's this young lady?"

"I'm Ian. Your place is amazing." I shake his large rough hand. "Can I pet Fancy?"

"Yes, but don't give her too many rinds. Makes her farts smell like rotting skunk. Jubal knows she sleeps in my room so he never visits without bringin' a bag."

The two men unload the feed from the back of the Blazer while I sit on the porch with Fancy. She takes the rinds gently. I try simple commands and find she is very smart. She can sit, lay, roll over and when I ignore her she pats my leg with her paw until I acknowledge her. I give her one, last pork rind and realize I need to eat, too. I walk around to the side of the house where the guys are.

"No. You listen. That's bad news. You know it and I know it. Your heart has always got you in trouble, man. Please, think about it." Jim has his hand on Jubal's shoulder trying to make sure his words reach him.

"Sorry to interrupt. I'm really hungry, Jubal." I pretend I don't hear them.

"She's always hungry. I hope you butchered enough cattle to fill her stomach." Jubal grins.

Jim looks at me then back at Jubal, clearly confused.

"I know she looks like a starved cat but she eats like a pig." He forces a laugh and they grab our bags from the Blazer and we go inside.

As soon as we step inside, my nostrils are flooded with the delicious aroma of barbecue. The inside of this place has a very masculine feel. It's very clean and simple. The chairs are overstuffed with a red plaid pattern. The couch is soft brown leather. There's a stone fireplace with an enormous moose's head mounted above the mantle. I follow Jim and Jubal into the kitchen and realize Jim has been preparing this feast all day. I'm close to drooling when Jim hands me a warm biscuit. "There's butter in the fridge. You can get the honey from the cupboard over there if you like them sweet. Dinner won't be ready for a bit longer."

"Thank you." I take the roll and breathe in the warm fresh aroma. I put on an impressive amount of butter but skip the honey.

"I'll show you to your room. You can freshen up in the bathroom across the hall. There's a brush in there if you'd like," Jim offers as he points to my messy coif.

Jubal cracks up laughing. I offer a half-amused, half-wounded laugh as Jim leads me down the hall.

The bedroom is small yet cozy. The twin bed has a fluffy down comforter and two large pillows. The dresser has six drawers with antique-looking handles. I laugh to myself. Everything I own is in my backpack. It'd be nice to have enough clothes to fill a dresser. The mirror above the dresser reflects a ratty looking little girl. I need more than a comb.

I open the door and call down for permission to shower before dinner. Jim tells me where to find a towel. I turn the shower to a nice, almost-too-hot-temperature and reach into my pack for a brush, shampoo and conditioner, clean undies and the only other outfit I own. Sweats and a *Muppet Show* t-shirt—great. I brush through my messy hair the best I can before stepping into the tub. The water feels wonderful. I'm thankful I packed my own toiletries because the only thing in the shower is a bottle of musky smelling, all in one shampoo-slash-body wash.

I dry off and brush through my hair. The

conditioner has helped a lot but there are still a ton of tangles. I never learned how to braid my hair, so I towel dry it and pull it into a ponytail. My clothes are clean, thanks to Jubal fixing the washing machine at the ranch house, but wrinkly from being stuffed in the bag. The steam from the shower has helped somewhat too. But I still look homeless.

I open the door and find Fancy waiting for me with a tattered Raggedy Ann doll in her mouth. Her tail is wagging and her back feet are dancing. She drops the doll and nudges it towards my feet. It's filthy. "Thank you, Fancy. Wanna play fetch?" I toss the doll into my room. Fancy turns but only goes over to pick the doll back up and then walks downstairs.

Once I put my pack into my room I go downstairs to ask Jim about the Raggedy Ann doll. "Hey, Jim? Fancy gave me her doll, but …" I'm frozen to the spot. In the kitchen with Jim and Jubal are two strangers along with a familiar face, all quietly staring at me.

"Well, that just means she likes you. Just tell her she's got a pretty baby and give it back to her. She's probably the only retriever who doesn't like to play fetch. These are my friends and farmhands, Marcus and Ricky. And, you've already met Sawyer." Jim smiles.

"Hi, everyone." I take a deep breath when they all go back to their conversations. I poke Jubal in the ribs with my thumb.

"Ouch. What's that for?"

"You knew he was gonna be here. You could've warned me."

"He said, 'See ya later', at the store. I figured you knew what *later* meant." He chuckles.

The dining room is also adorned with dead animal heads. I don't mind them. I just don't like eating with them looking at me. The table has a serious amount of food on it. I promise myself I will try everything. First things, first—I grab some ribs.

I keep staring at Sawyer. His light brown hair hangs in waves. His lips are full. I even notice his hands, as he brings the fork to his mouth. Before I can look away, he catches me. He just smiles and if his lips weren't captivating enough, his smile and deep dimples bring instant warmth to my cheeks.

"You've got a little barbecue sauce on your face." Jubal nudges my arm with a grin.

I bury my face in my napkin. I've been staring at Sawyer like a weirdo with food all over my face. I stomp hard on Jubal's foot under the table. He cries out.

"Jim, please tell me you made your famous cobbler. I've been dreaming about that stuff for months now." Jubal licks his lips in anticipation.

"It wasn't me who stayed away so long."

"I know, brother. I know. I said sorry a hundred times, man."

Sawyer tries to change the subject by asking Jubal about his Harley. Jim gets up from the table and disappears into the kitchen. I'm hoping he went to get the cobbler. I'm finishing up the last couple bites of baked beans on my plate, and wondering if he has ice cream to go with dessert.

Jim returns with the yummiest blueberry cobbler I've ever had. Although, comparing this to school cafeteria food isn't fair. The table is silent while everyone cleans their plates of every last bite of the blueberry gooeyness.

"Thanks, Jim. I'm beat and we're gonna have an early morning. Good night, everyone." Marcus excuses himself from the table and heads into the kitchen with his plates. Ricky follows.

"Jubal, what're we doing tomorrow?"

"We ain't doin' anything. I have to go out of town and you'll be staying here with Jim."

"Actually, the guys and I'll be at the auction in Milton. So, you'll have the place to yourself." Jim speaks through a yawn.

I force a smile and offer to wash the dishes. Sawyer insists on helping. Jim and Jubal head into the living room while Sawyer and I clear the table.

"So, how do you know Jubal?" Sawyer asks while scraping plates into a plastic tub he brought in from the porch.

"He's a friend."

"Where are you from?"

"Nevada. How do you know them?"

"Jim is a longtime friend of the family. He was in the army with my dad. Jubal used to come around a lot more. But it's always nice to see him. His laugh is hilarious. He taught me a lot about cars. He actually helped me work on my truck."

"I don't know what I'd do without him."

"Where are your parents?"

"They died. I don't like to talk about it."

"I'm sorry. Hey, do you wanna go fishing tomorrow?"

"Where? Indigo Lake? I think I should make sure it's okay with Jubal. But, I'd like that."

A half-hour later we join the guys in the living room. Again, I get the feeling Jim has been lecturing Jubal.

"We took the leftovers out to the pigs. I'm gonna call it a night. Thanks for a great meal, Jim. Jubal, would it be okay if I take Ian fishing tomorrow?"

I blush instantly and stare at the wall when Jubal looks at me. I don't mind Sawyer asking Jubal, I just wasn't ready for it. Jubal looks back to Sawyer and nods his approval.

"Great. I'll pick you up at four."

"Four? As in, a.m.?"

Jubal and Sawyer laugh, but Jim just wishes us *good night* and heads upstairs. "Come on, Fancy." She picks up her Raggedy Ann and follows him to bed.

"Good night, Sawyer." Jubal locks the door and returns to the living room. He rubs his hand over his bald head. I'm not sure if he's tired or upset.

I sit in the recliner next to him and continue the question game we played earlier. "How is Jim your brother? You said we were coming to see your brother."

"Jim is my brother. We grew up in the same foster home. Well, I was in two other ones before I met Jim. He showed me what family means, man. That's why I don't get…"

Jubal stops and rubs his head some more.

"Are flip-flops okay for fishing?" I ask Jubal. He nods. "Why's Jim so upset with you?" I know it's not my turn, but I try anyway.

"Pass." Jubal stands up, takes three steps, before turning his head over his shoulder in my direction. "I'll see you when I get back. We'll get you some shoes and a few outfits then. G'night."

I find myself alone—just me, and the enormous moose. Sawyer pops into my head. It occurs to me we'll be spending the day together tomorrow. Just the two of us. I suddenly wish I could trade places with the moose.

I turn lights off, get a glass of water, and head to my room. There are two t-shirts folded on the edge of my bed. I open one to see an American flag on the top left with *Freedom Farms* in bold font below it. The right sleeve reads, "One Nation Under God". One is a size small and the other a large. Jim must've left them for me––one to wear, and the other to sleep in.

Four o'clock will be here way too soon. I crawl into bed and drift off, succumbing easily. *My mom walks into my room. She sits on my bed and pets my hair. She is whispering something but I can't understand her. I turn the small lamp on so I can see her. She has a busted lip and her left eye is swollen shut. I know what happened to her but I ask anyway, "Who did this to you?" She continues petting my hair but is much rougher, pulling strands from my scalp. "You did this to me, Ian. You did this."*

I sit upright, panting. Beads of sweat make their way down my neck. There's a soft tapping at my bedroom door. I turn my head wildly, searching my room for any sign my mother was here. Nothing. There wouldn't be. She wasn't here. It was just a dream. A bad dream.

Jubal opens the door and sits on the edge of my bed. "It's almost four. You okay?"

"Bad dream."

"Well, you're safe now. I'll let Sawyer know you'll be down in a few minutes. I better get going. Here's a key. Jim and his guys have already left. I'll be back late tonight. Here's forty bucks in case you need anything." Jubal closes the door behind him.

Sawyer is in the kitchen pouring me some coffee. "I hope it tastes better than that stuff Jubal brews. I thought my heart was going to explode."

"Good morning. Here." The mug Sawyer hands me warms me instantly. I'm not sure if it's the heat from the cup or his hand touching mine.

"Let's go. Do we need chairs? I saw some out back when we took the pigs their slop bucket."

"Chairs? We'll be on the boat."

"Oh. Okay. I thought we'd be on the beach." Suddenly I'm wishing I'd said no. Sawyer opens my door for me. He points things out to me along the way: The mini mart that has the most flavors of slushies. His old high school, a large two-story brick building. He also points out the ski lifts, and offers to take me skiing if I visit in the winter. "I've never skied, but I'm excited to try. Jubal promised to bring me back." I know the lake is to the right of us, but it's still too dark to see. Sawyer slows the truck and turns in to the drive of *The Indigo Yacht Club.* "You have a *yacht?*" I blurt out.

"No. My parents have a boat. There are all kinds and sizes of boats moored here."

I pull the hood over my head and wish my toes weren't so cold. The early morning air is chilling. We walk along the dock, passing beautiful boats and some old smaller ones. The sun is beginning to lighten the sky.

"Good morning, Sawyer. Who's your friend?" A very old woman smoking a very smelly pipe greets us with a wrinkly hand.

"Morning, Ms. June. This is Ian."

"Don't jinx my catch, Miss Ian." Her yellow smile fades as she passes us.

"What's she mean by that?" I look to Sawyer, who is giggling quietly.

"She's old school… very superstitious. Believes outsiders attract the fish. It's not personal. She's actually very nice."

"Let's hope she's right, then." I smile.

Chapter Five

Sawyer stops in front of a very beautiful boat that bears the name *Atticus* in large bold blue letters. I stand there taking in its enormity while he steps aboard. There are several dark windows along the length of the boat and pin-striping in the same blue as the letters.

"Are you coming?" Sawyer is standing there with an outstretched hand waiting for me to step aboard.

"This is *so* not just a boat! It's enormous! Do you even know how to drive it?"

"I'm not driving. I thought *you* were driving!" He laughs his fantastic laugh, and I feel the warmth in my chest as I take his hand.

"You are *so* funny," I say in a sarcastic tone.

I follow Sawyer up a few steps into a small room with two seats and a steering wheel. He tells me to have a seat and heads back down the steps. I watch him as he hops over, pulls the fat rope from the dock, and plops down in the seat next to me.

"Here we go." Sawyer guides us through the rows of boats and into the open water.

The scenery around us is breathtaking. The lake is so big I can't see the end of it. The yacht club and surrounding beaches disappear behind us. I can see Sawyer sneaking glances my way.

"Can you go faster?"

"Hold on!" Sawyer laughs and pushes a lever forward, propelling us through the water with a rise and fall of the waves.

I'm lost in laughter and exhilaration. I've never felt so weightless before. Sawyer drives us a while, before the engines stop.

"Did you break it? Why aren't we moving?"

"No, I didn't break it! This is where we're going to fish. Come on. I'll give you a tour." Sawyer leads me downstairs.

I'm in shock. There is a house inside the boat. There's a kitchen, dining area and sleeping quarters. It's small but elegant. I turn to look inside the bathroom and my right flip-flop snaps.

"Oh, shit!" A levee of emotion crumbles inside my chest and I'm on my knees sobbing.

Sawyer kneels down next to me and puts his arm under mine, lifting me to my feet so I can sit on the bed. "It's okay."

"No, it's not okay. The stupid cokeheads took my shoes at the river and these flip-flops were the only other shoes I had." Sawyer sits next to me, holding me and petting my hair in silence.

I stop crying and the reality of my embarrassment hits me hard in the pit of my stomach. I wipe my tears on my sleeve and take a deep breath. "Can you please take me back to Jim's?"

"Why? Look, I'm sure there are some water shoes around here you can put on. We still have a great day ahead of us." He's up before I can say no. "Here, try these on. I have a nice lunch in the fridge for us and you haven't proven Ms. June right yet."

The shoes are horrid. White rubber soles with purple and orange mesh tops. They are probably two sizes too big. I just say thank you and wipe my nose on my sleeve again.

Sawyer holds out his hand and walks to the stairs. My feet stumble in the big shoes so Sawyer tightens his grip to steady me. I feel both thankful and humiliated. How is it that he can calm me down with such ease? He's nice. That's why.

Sawyer stops in front of the seats lining each side of the boat. He lifts the cushions to reveal fishing gear. Sawyer hands me a pole and has one leaning on the seat beside him. He pulls out a small Styrofoam bowl of night crawlers and looks at me with a toothy grin. "Want me to hook your worm?"

"No way! I'll watch you first so I know what to do."

Sawyer takes a long worm and pinches it between his thumb and pointer finger, severing it in half with his fingernail. He hands me one half and begins to thread the other half on his hook. It looks disgusting. I can't wait to try it.

"I'm impressed." Sawyer compliments me, then continues. "Okay, now stand here. Take the rod in your right hand. Flip this thing down while holding the string with your pointer finger. Raise it like this and give it a flick. Now flip this back up and you've just completed your very first cast."

I don't remember any of the instructions because he's standing so close to me and guiding my movements with his hands. I'll have to pay attention to what he does.

"So, how will I know if I catch one?"

"You'll feel the fish bite."

"They have *teeth*?"

"No!" Sawyer is laughing wildly. "They'll swallow the hook and it'll tug the rod. It's like a bunch of little tugs. When you feel it just jerk the rod to hook the fish. Then you wind it in a little and wait, then wind again. You keep winding until you reel it in."

Just as Sawyer finishes his instruction, my pole starts to vibrate in my hand. I scream in excitement. I follow his steps and reel in a decent-sized fish. Its silver scales shine in the sunlight.

"It's huge! Grab it!" I'm hopping from one foot to the other in excitement. I can barely control myself.

Sawyer and I struggle to grab the slippery fish, but just as the hook is loose it slips from our grasp and splashes into the water. I turn on Sawyer and strike him in the arm. "You let it go! You did that on purpose!"

"It was your fish. You let it get away." Sawyer nudges my arm, causing me to lose my balance in the oversized shoes. He catches me. Actually, it's more like I fall into him.

I look into his brown eyes and before I can stop myself, I'm kissing him. It's not like the time in seventh grade when Chad kissed me in the empty locker room. It's a kiss like you see in the movies.

"Whoa. Whoa. Whoa." Sawyer pulls away from me.

"Oh my gosh. I'm so sorry. Must be all the adrenaline from catching a fish." For a second, I think about jumping overboard to join my escaped fish.

"It's okay. You just caught me by surprise."

I dig in for a worm and throw my line in without another word. Despite it being just a decent cast, Sawyer makes a very big deal about it. I know he's trying to make me feel better. I decide to get over it and enjoy the afternoon. We fish for a few more hours. Sawyer catches several fish but throws most of them back. He keeps two nice size trout in a cooler. I catch a few very small fish and I'm happy to throw them back.

"Are you hungry? I'm hungry." Sawyer puts our poles back under the cushions and we go inside to wash up and eat.

Sawyer has brought us a delicious salad with seasoned chicken, mandarin oranges and a spicy ginger dressing. I practically lick my plate.

"Sawyer, I'm sorry about earlier. I was pretty aggressive."

"I think you bit me." Sawyer chuckles as he checks the inside of his lip for blood. "Really, it's okay."

"Ha, ha. I wasn't *that* bad." I throw my napkin at him, but he catches it.

When we pull into the driveway at Jim's we see him unloading a beautiful horse from his trailer. He has a proud look on his face as he waves us over.

"Oh, Jim! She's beautiful." Sawyer joins Jim, Marcus and Ricky at the trailer.

I go straight to my room and replace the horrid water shoes with a clean pair of socks. When I get to the front door I see Sawyer driving away. I want to return the water shoes but I'm relieved I don't have to face him. I think I've had enough embarrassment for one day.

"Sawyer wanted me to let you know he'll try to stop back by before you leave. He had to go help his dad. Jubal says you know how to cook. Do you mind making supper? I need to help the guys get Lulu settled in." Jim's smiling from ear to ear.

"I'd love to. Is Lulu the lady you've had your eyes on for a while now? I thought Marcus was talking about an actual woman."

"They like to tease me, but Lulu is a beautiful creature. I'll be in to help you as soon as I finish up."

"She's a pretty horse. Don't worry about dinner. I can handle it."

The house is quiet. I open the back door and sit on the deck watching him walk Lulu around her new pen. Fancy joins me. The sun is setting behind the trees. The colors in the sky are relaxing. I get up to check on dinner and find Sawyer in the kitchen.

"Holy shit! You scared me."

"I'm sorry. I just wanted to drop these off with you and say goodbye." Sawyer sets a box on the table. He's bought me a pair of shoes.

"Sawyer, you didn't have to do that."

"Fine. I'll take them back." He picks up the Converse box and turns to leave.

"Wait! At least let me look at 'em…"

"No. You don't want them. I'll just return them." He teases me with a crooked grin.

I chase him into the living room and tackle him on the ottoman. The box tumbles to the floor. We are a tangled mess of arms and legs. I'm laughing, trying to reach the shoes. Sawyer is pulling my arms just shy of reaching them without much effort. Jim walks in and clears his throat. "What's going on in here?"

"Hey, Jim. Just brought Ian some shoes. She broke her flip-flop on the boat. I felt I owed her some new shoes, but she is *not* interested."

"That's not true!" I kick free and grab the shoes and their box.

"Those are some nice shoes, Ian." Jim stands there fully entertained.

"Oh no! Dinner." I drop the box and slide into the kitchen.

"Will you be joining us, Sawyer?" Jim asks as they appear in the kitchen.

"No, I better get goin'. My mom is expecting me. I made the Dean's list again. She makes a big deal of it."

"As she should. I'm very proud of you, Sawyer. You tell them I said hello and thank him for the saddle blanket. I'm goin' to go wash up." Jim leaves with a wave.

Sawyer walks around the kitchen table and comes in close to me. I love the way he smells. He stands there like he's trying to think of the right words but can't. Finally, he speaks.

"I had fun with you. It's been a long time since I've been fishing. Thank you." He pulls me in for a hug and kisses the top of my head.

"Thank you for taking me. I had a great time. I hope we can come back so you can take me skiing." I look into his eyes, willing him to kiss me. "And thank you for my shoes."

"You're welcome. I better go."

He walks to the kitchen door and turns to me. "Can I call you?"

"I'd like that a lot." It's not a kiss, but the butterflies in my tummy have awakened.

The table is set and I'm putting the food out when Marcus and Ricky come in. They take their seats, placing their napkins in their laps. Jim and Fancy join us and we dig in. The guys praise my cooking. I'm pleased when they help themselves to seconds.

"Is there dessert, Ian?" Marcus asks with hopeful eyes.

"Um, no. I didn't get a chance to make dessert." *Too busy horseplaying with Sawyer.*

"That's all right. I don't have any place to put it anyhow. I better call it a good night." Ricky tries to make me feel better but there's something in his voice that makes me think Jim always has dessert.

I join Jim in the living room after I clean up the kitchen and find he's building a fire. It's not cold enough to need one but he tells me it relaxes him. I agree. I love watching the flames.

"Jim? I know you think Jubal having me around is a bad idea. I just want you to know that I'd never do anything to get him in trouble. He's looked out for me from the first time we saw each other. I care about him so much."

"That's nice of you to say. Jubal is a good one. But, I wasn't talking about you. I've wanted him to get away from Mikus from day one. He's bad news. You watch your back around that guy. I'm pretty good at reading people. Damn good, actually. Even if I get a bad feeling about someone I give 'em the benefit of the doubt. Mikus burned me the first chance he got."

"What happened?" I'm so interested in his story I can feel my body move closer to his so I can hear the words sooner.

"Our foster parents were an older couple who didn't have kids of their own. They really latched on to the two of us. They didn't have much but they left us their wedding bands and our dad left us each a pocket watch. They were old. He worked for a watchmaker when he was a boy. The two watches were his attempts. They didn't work but he kept them his entire life. I had them here. Jubal brought Mikus to meet me and they stayed the weekend. He stole them. He sat at my table and ate my food, and he stole from me. Man, I really don't like him."

"What did Jubal say?"

"He never knew. I cornered Mikus on the side of the house and made the little Irish thug shake in his boots until he finally handed them back over to me. I didn't tell Jubal. It wouldn't matter. Mikus would've spun a story to make Jubal believe he was misunderstood."

"How did you two turn out so different? Jubal isn't a bad guy but he isn't as grounded as you. He talks about you a lot. He always says *Yeah, my brother this* or *my brother that*. He looks up to you."

"I don't know how much he's told you but we

both had a rough start. I was lucky enough to be placed with the Welsh's when I was seven. Jubal, on the other hand, was bounced around a bit more. He's a tough guy but he got that way because of the bullshit he went through as a young boy. His first foster father was strict and his second was very abusive, both physically and mentally. By the time he came to me, he was defeated. He wouldn't talk for almost six months. We had to work hard to show him what love means. What family means."

"Jubal told me how he became friends with Mikus. I don't like him either. He has scary eyes. Jubal told me he has just a little while longer to wait and he can save enough for his garage." Just thinking about Mikus makes me nervous, like he can somehow hear me talking about him. A shiver runs up my spine.

"That's the thing, Ian. He doesn't need any more money. I own the garage."

"You *do*? Why then?" I can't believe it.

"He's too proud. He says I've helped him too much. He's always relied on me. He has to do this his way. I accept that. I just wish he'd do it without Mikus."

"Are you rich?"

"No, I'm not rich." Jim laughs. "I have worked my ass off for every last thing I have. I joined the Army and saved every penny earned. When I got out I bought this piece of land and lived in a nasty little travel trailer that stunk to high Heaven for three years while I built this house. I slowly built my farm to what you see today."

"I didn't mean to upset you. I really think your place is wonderful. You should be proud of your hard work. Why didn't Jubal come to you when he got out of jail?"

"I honestly think Mikus uses Jubal. He exploits his kindhearted nature. I asked him a million times to join me here at Freedom Farms. When I left our foster home he made me a promise that he'd behave and become a man I could be proud of. I guess he's still trying to keep that promise. He doesn't see that I am proud of him already."

I can see why Jubal loves Jim so much. I wish we didn't have to go back to Cavern Creek. But if Jubal says he only has a little while longer, I can stick it out. I make a mental note to be as invisible as possible when Mikus is around. I'll keep the peace until the day Jubal has enough savings to make his dream come true.

Jim makes some hot tea for himself and a glass of chocolate milk for me. I'm curled up on the couch with a blanket watching the fire cast shadows around the room, making the moose appear to come alive. It's very unsettling.

"I take it you and Sawyer hit it off? Now, *there* is a good kid. He worked hard to finish high school early and get into college. He's a good one, all right."

"I can't believe he bought me shoes. That was so nice. And I was a total mess. I kissed him. I don't know what got into me. I've never done anything like that. He's such a nice guy. And he's so cute."

We talk a little while longer, then sit in silence and enjoy the glow of the fire. He stays up after I tell him good night. I hug him and he returns the hug. I thank him for being a good man. I'm glad to know he doesn't hate me or wish I wasn't around.

I fall asleep thinking about my day with Sawyer. He must follow me into sleep because I dream about him. Jubal comes in sometime before the sun comes up. At first I think he's part of my dream but he moves my bangs from my eyes and whispers *Good night.* I'm relieved he made it back safely. I missed him too.

TRACI JO STOTTS

Chapter Six

"Good morning, Jubal!" I slide across the kitchen floor and give him a big hug.

"*You kissed Sawyer?*" Jubal is smiling his huge smile.

"Jim!" I turn bright red. I planned on telling Jubal all about it, but him knowing already is very embarrassing.

"You never said it was a secret." He laughs into his coffee cup.

"It's not a secret. I just thought I'd get a *good morning* and maybe have the option of telling him myself." I nudge Jim as I reach for a coffee cup.

Jim has made a great breakfast of waffles, eggs, fried potatoes and bacon, and I load my plate. I hate the thought of leaving this place and going back to the ranch. Going back to Mikus. "When are we leaving, Jubal?"

"As soon as you finish eating. We should've left already." Jubal gets up to rinse his plate.

"Jubal, can you come out back with me? I'd like you to meet Lulu." Jim gives me a wink and steps out the back door.

"Make sure you're all packed. I'd hate for you to forget your brand new shoes."

"Jim!" I yell in his direction. He just laughs his reply.

I go upstairs to get my backpack. I can see the guys leaning on the gate. Jim is talking to Jubal who is petting Lulu's black mane. I slowly slide the window open because I'm dying to hear what he's saying. When I hear, I'm glad I opened the window.

"You've got a very special girl in there. You take care of her. And don't wait so long before coming to see your brother. I miss you, man." Jim hugs Jubal for a long while before letting go.

We throw our bags in the Blazer and I'm hanging out the window waving wildly to Jim and Fancy as Jubal drives away. We ride along in silence. I think he hates leaving Jim as much as I do.

Jubal stops at Mervyn's so I can pick out some clothes. I go straight to the clearance racks. I pick out two pairs of jeans and four tops. I tell Jubal it's more than enough but he reminds me that I've been washing my undergarments every two days. He points at a cute jean jacket. "You need a coat. Do you like this?"

"I love it. But I have my hoodie. This is already a lot of money."

"You're doing a great job helping around the house and in the garage. You're earning these clothes. Now, try it on and stop being a pain in my ass." He laughs and tosses the coat over my head.

We don't play the question game on the way home. Instead we turn the radio up and sing along to Casey Kasem's Top 40 Countdown. If one of us forgets the lyrics we make them up as we go. I love his laughter and the sparkle in his eyes. The trip flies by.

We pull into the garage and Mikus is pacing. His bright red hair is a wild mess and he is sweating like crazy. Jubal tells me to go straight inside and lock myself in his room. I don't argue. Once inside I turn the television on and flip through channels until Doris Day is singing "The Windy City" from *Calamity Jane*. I love her movies. I try to stop my mind from trying to figure out what is going on in the garage at this very moment. I don't care.

"Ian. Wake up. Mikus is in trouble. We have to go to Reno for a few. I don't have time to put the lock on your room so you can stay in here. I wrote the number to

Sylvia's. If there's an emergency, call. Only in an emergency. Otherwise, I'll be back as soon as I can." Jubal is emptying his bag and pulling clean clothes from the drawers to fill it again.

"Why do you have to clean up his mess?" I sit up rubbing my eyes, wondering how long I've been sleeping. I look out the window at the dark sky and realize they must've been coming up with a plan for hours.

"Don't! Don't you go all Jim on me! You will not question me about Mikus." Jubal tries to calm his tone but it's too late.

I bury my face in the blanket to hide my tears. "I'm sorry. I didn't mean…"

"I know you didn't mean to. I don't have time for this right now. Don't be mad at me. I'll be back before you know it. I'll call you when I can."

"Are you going to be okay?" My words come out broken. I don't want him to leave when he's mad at me.

"Come here." Jubal opens his arms and I'm in them before he can change his mind.

The roar of their bikes rattles me to the core. I hate being in this house. I miss Jim and Fancy. I miss Ricky and Marcus. I miss Sawyer. I run down to the kitchen and heat up a frozen dinner and find some crackers and peanut butter. I check all of the locks and take the food and a big cup of chocolate milk upstairs and lock myself inside Jubal's room. I don't want to be in this house alone, and definitely not at night.

I flip through the channels on the television and stop on *The Love Boat*. Julie is helping a newlywed couple work through a heated argument about his wandering eye. Julie reminds me of my mother with her short sandy blonde hair, and blue eyes. I am not willing to let myself think about my parents. I kick my legs over the side of the bed and open the drawer of the nightstand looking for a pen and some paper. I see some foot fungal cream and an outdated *TV Guide*. There's also a half pack of gum and a package of condoms. "Oh, gross."

I unlock the bedroom door and go downstairs to look for the tablet with Sylvia's number on it. Jubal said it was by the phone. The second step creeks and my pulse races. I tell myself to stop being a baby. Two deep breaths … Nope, that didn't work. I grab the tablet and pen and I'm back in Jubal's room locking the deadbolt in seconds. Once I'm sitting on the bed I bust out into laughter. I've slept on the riverbank with crackheads all around me. I am being ridiculous.

My mind is flooded with the faces of my parents, Jim, Fancy, and Jubal and Sawyer. I focus on one. I want to write to Sawyer but I don't know what to say to him. He's so great and I'm just a little girl who has a crush on him. I'll just wait and hope he calls me like he said he would. For now, I start a letter to Jim. I tell him how nice it was to be in his comfortable home, how thankful I am for the Freedom Farms shirts and how I promise to help Jubal save up enough to get out of here. Out of here, and far away from Mikus.

The sun shines through the window so brightly I wake with squinted eyes. I look around to figure out where I am and where Jubal is. I'm irritated when I remember I'm alone here in this place for a few days. I drag myself out of bed and head downstairs. Strangely enough, I want coffee.

I grab the coffee pot to add water and notice the thick brown ring from probably a thousand pots of coffee being brewed and never washed. I reach for the dish soap and a scouring pad. There are several bottles of different cleaners. Most are brand new. Boys are gross. After I scrub the coffee pot to a brilliant shine, I notice the grimy dirt all over the counters and sink. The entire kitchen is a mess. I clean up every day, but this is the first deep cleaning. I'm disgusted.

Hours pass and I have scrubbed every nook and cranny of the downstairs. The bathroom was so disgusting I had to spray it down with cleaner and let it sit for a while before tackling the nastiness in there. I'm pretty sure I've earned my keep today. I emptied a bottle of dusting spray, a box of scrubby pads and a bar of soap from washing my hands a million times.

I take the trash outside and walk over to the garage. The tools are all in place. The workspace is clean and tidy on Jubal's side. Mikus' side is as messy as his red hair. The hoses are wound into neat round nests. The push brooms are leaning in the corner beside the floor compound. If they cleaned up after themselves in the house like they do out here, I wouldn't have spent the entire day on my hands and knees scrubbing layers of dirt from the floors.

I glance over at the Blazer. It's pretty dirty. I can't think of anything better to do so I grab the hose and a bucket. The hose doesn't reach. I get the keys from Jubal's nightstand and after setting them down and picking them back up three times, I'm sitting in the driver's seat and the engine is running. I pull the seat forward so I can reach the pedals and realize I can't quite see over the steering wheel. I curl my left leg under my butt and sit on my foot. It works. I can see.

After a few deep breaths I move the shifter into reverse and ease it out of the garage. I step on the brake, too hard. I'm jolted in my seat. I yank the shifter into park. After containing my laughter and collecting myself, I shift into drive and edge forward towards the garden hose. The adrenaline rushing through me is exciting. I can't help myself. I drive around the house once, slowly. The second time around I drive a bit faster. After circling the house twice, without causing damage to myself or the vehicle, I venture out and drive all over the property. The windows are down and the radio is up. I follow a dirt road behind the garage that leads to a separate gate. I drive back and park by the hose before I'm tempted to leave.

I'm beyond tired. The house is spotless. The Blazer is sparkling. Another night alone in this house is punishment. I make some toast and crawl into bed. I pick up the remote and surf through the channels but nothing is on. I click off the TV, and drift off thinking of the day on the lake. I can see Sawyer's face and hear his laughter like he's in the room with me. I wish that was true.

~~~~~~~~

I'm up before the sun. Grouchy. I grab the broom and sweep the porch. I hear the rumbling of the motorcycles and finish sweeping the porch and run down the steps to the garage.

"You drove the Blazer?" Jubal asks as he pulls off his helmet.

"I moved it so I can wash it. I've been so bored."

"Jubal, I meant what I said." Mikus walks quickly by me and slams the screen door behind him. I wonder if he appreciates the clean house. Probably doesn't even notice.

"It looks great." Jubal has the door open and is checking out the inside of his Blazer.

"Seriously, I was so bored. There is nothing to eat in there, so if you want dinner, we better run to the store."

"Hop in!" Jubal is happy and smiling. I'm glad he's not mad at me for driving. I apologize anyway.

We load up on groceries. Jubal informs me that he'll be making dinner tonight and he makes the "best jalapeno stuffed burgers on the planet". I have never had anything other than a regular burger so I am looking forward to it. Two people stop and say hey to Jubal.

"Hey, Julie. Hi, Joe. This is Ian. She's Mikus' cousin." He points to me and I stare at the floor. My face is red with embarrassment and shock. I guess it makes sense, as he can't tell the world he's harboring a runaway. It still makes me uncomfortable.

"That was cold, Jubal!" I hit Jubal in his arm. He just laughs and continues to load the cart.

We get home and unload the groceries. Jubal notices the house right when he walks in. I love the praise he gives me. Mikus just rolls his eyes and grabs a beer. We tell Mikus what we're making for dinner. He tries to be unimpressed but his eyes light up at the mention of Jubal's amazing burgers.

"I'm going to make German chocolate cake. Jubal says it's your favorite." Mikus just grunts and leaves the room. I'm defeated.

"Finish putting these away. I'll be right back." Jubal follows him out of the room.

I stand by the doorway trying to hear what they are talking about. At first, I can't make out a single word. But then they become a little louder. I can hear the strain in Jubal's tone.

"Fine. If she goes, I go."

That's what Mikus meant when they first got home. He wants me gone. I'm about to put my two cents in when Jubal storms in. "I said put the food away."

"I'm sorry. Jubal, I never meant to start a fight."

"I know. It's not your fault. He knows I can't go anywhere anyway. I had to use most of my savings to bail him out. Again."

"You had to *what*?" Just as I asked, Mikus walks in. I avoid making any eye contact with him.

"Look, Jubal. We're partners." He moves his hands from his chest towards Jubal. "I made a mistake. It won't happen again. But we ain't baby sitters."

"Ian takes better care of herself than you do, man. What's your problem? Look at this place. It's never been this clean. I stand by what I said: if you want her gone, we both go." Jubal steps out back to light the barbeque.

I can feel the daggers Mikus is staring into me. I force myself to look him in the eyes. "What can I do to make this work? I don't want to leave."

"You'll leave. One way or another, you'll leave." Mikus throws his empty can towards the garbage but misses. He gives me a you-can-clean-that-up smirk, grabs another beer from the fridge and leaves the kitchen.

I pick up the can and toss it in the garbage. "What a jerk." The words come out as a whisper but in my head I'm screaming. I get a bowl and put the ingredients on the table. Jubal comes back in and shows me how he makes these mouthwatering tear-inducing burgers.

"You've gotta be careful not to rub your eyes after touching these peppers. I know from experience. It's not pretty."

I'm relieved he's not in a bad mood. While Jubal forms the hamburger into patties, I prepare the cake mix. I'm half tempted to sneeze in the bowl. "How are you going to get your money back?"

"I don't want to talk about it. Just know there'll be a lot more trips to Reno in the near future. You like to read? We can go into town and get some books from the secondhand store. Maybe they have some of them Doris Day movies you like so much."

I want to stomp my feet and throw a tantrum but I know it's not the time and it definitely won't help my case. The thought of being here alone again puts me in a grouchy mood. "I wish you had a dog. I can't stand being alone."

"I'm trying to get Mikus to be okay with you being here, and you're trying to add to the mess!" Jubal waves his spatula at me.

By the time Jubal has his burgers off the grill and the cake is cooling, Mikus comes in and appears to have a pretty decent buzz. The three of us sit together at the kitchen table. Mikus is sharing stories and actually being pretty decent to me. I like this version of Mikus. I laugh at his jokes and when he slides a beer my way, I accept. Jubal raises his eyes, but doesn't object. The Bud Light tastes delicious. I find myself wondering why I never snuck a beer from my parents. The thought of my mother and father makes it impossible to swallow the liquid in my mouth. Suddenly, the beer tastes like bleach.

The burgers are truly mouthwatering. I let Mikus cut the cake so he can get the biggest piece. I'm tempted to make another burger but choose dessert instead.

"You did good on the house. Is this your life's goal? To become a maid?" Mikus doesn't have a rude tone to the question. He's just making conversation.

"No. I'm gonna work with Jubal. I plan on taking business classes and working the books in his garage. I'm pretty good with numbers." I turn the beer in circles but do not take another drink.

"Pretty good with numbers, huh?" Mikus is looking at me through curious eyes. I can almost see the light bulb illuminate above his head.

"Mikus, I think we should call it a night. We gotta get to Sylvia's before nine." Jubal stands and collects the empty plates and beer bottles.

"I think a clean house is great. But, hear me out." Mikus is looking from me to Jubal and back at me. "Just look at her, Jubal. So cute and innocent… I bet she could make a drop right in front of a cop and not get noticed."

"Man. How many times do I gotta tell you? It ain't happening." Jubal's jaw barely moves. The veins in his neck are thick and full.

"Fine. I'll drop it. For now." Mikus grabs two beers from the fridge and heads to his room.

Jubal looks at me but I can't read his face. I know he's furious with Mikus. He tells me to go to bed while he takes care of the dishes.

"I'm not afraid, Jubal."

"Go."

"Jubal, I'll do anything to help you."

"*I said go!*" Jubal yells.

I crawl into bed with tears running down my face. I know Jubal isn't mad at me. He's just mad at Mikus. But it hurts that he doesn't want my help. Mikus keeps taking his money and pushing his dreams farther out of reach.

Chapter Seven

It's been four months without any more talk of me delivering for Mikus. In fact, he's back to despising my very existence. The only time he is halfway decent is when he's got a killer buzz going. Needless to say, I keep him in steady supply of beer.

I've gotten good at reading his moods. He still scares the shit out of me but I stick up for myself. After Jubal broke up a pretty gnarly argument between me and Mikus, he came up with a plan to keep me out of Mikus' hair. He asked me to follow him to the garage where he pointed to an old motorcycle, or more like a skeleton of one. He told me I could have it once I've built it. I've been in the garage every day since.

"Ian! Phone," Mikus hollers from the screen door.

I get phone calls from two people: Jim or Sawyer. It doesn't matter which one is on the line—I'm sprinting to the receiver.

"How'd you like to go fishing tomorrow?" Sawyer's voice is filled with excitement.

"Jubal and Mikus are on their way to Reno in a few minutes. I still don't have my license." I put extra emphasis on the last part. Jubal has a friend at the DMV who owes him a favor so he's going to take me to get my license. I have all the proper documentation, but he never has the time.

"I mean, I'll come to you. We can fish on the Lutz."

"Is that your dad's other boat?"

"No!" Sawyer bursts with laughter. "It's the river there in Cavern Creek. I finished my finals and I want to celebrate. With you."

"Let me make sure it's okay with Jubal. Hold on." I drop the receiver on the counter and run into the living room.

Mikus is sitting on the coffee table with his tote bags of drugs, waiting for Jubal. I turn towards the hallway to find Jubal when Mikus laughs his eerie laugh. "Make sure he brings condoms. I may have a hard time gettin' you outta here, but I draw the line at bastard babies."

"Don't be gross, Mikus. It's not like that."

"The hell it ain't! You get on the phone with him and your voice gets all *high*, like this. You giggle your slutty giggle. I ain't stupid." Mikus is giving his best impression of a girl.

"I beg to differ." Mikus doesn't hear me through his laughter.

Jubal looks at me trying to decide whether or not I need *The Talk*. He lists off a million rules before giving me his approval. I rush back to the phone and tell Sawyer, who informs me he'll be here tonight so we can get to the river early. I like this idea. I hate being here alone.

Jubal comes into the garage with Mikus behind him. "We'll be back in two days. I expect a fish fry when we get back."

"Be safe," Mikus says, and explodes into laughter.

Their bikes roar to life before I can tell Mikus to shove it up his ass. They drive off leaving a dust trail. My focus is no longer on my bike. I decide to make a sandwich and sit on the porch. It's a good thing I'm so small. The swing doesn't look like it can hold much weight.

Mikus' ranch could be beautiful with a little TLC. I remind myself to ask him how many acres his place sits on. I need to ask when he's in a friendly mood or he'll probably think I want to steal it from under him. He can be so paranoid.

The Haynes manual is my teacher when Jubal is gone. I flip through the pages while humming along with the radio. I'm clamping the bars to the forks when the hair stands up on the back of my neck. I hear the crunching sound of footsteps approaching me. I know it's not Sawyer. It's more than one person. I grab a screwdriver and squeeze it tightly and turn to see three men. One is walking up to me while other two are standing by the car.

"Easy, Chica. I don't want to fight you." The stranger smiles and raises his hands.

"What do you want?"

"I'm looking for Mikus."

"He's not here. I can go inside and get Jubal. Maybe he knows where you can find him."

"No. It's okay. You just tell him Julio came by. You tell him he's behind on payments. This time is a courtesy call." He smiles again.

I want to vomit.

The second the car is out of sight I run inside and lock the doors. I sit by the front windows for a while until I feel comfortable they are gone for good. I don't consider this an emergency but I can't wait for Jubal to call me.

I turn the TV on because the silence is making me nervous. Sawyer should be here in a few hours. *Family Feud* is on and Richard Dawson is flirting with all the ladies. What a pervert. I shout out my guesses and play along with the Fast Money round. I love watching the family members high-five each other and I cheer them on even when their guesses are stupid.

I clean up the house and make a simple casserole for dinner. Mikus has a collection of cookbooks from the

50's. The covers are outdated but I've tried several recipes and they've all been good. I shouldn't say all … I cooked a maple Dijon chicken that had to be choked down. Jubal was nice and said they can't all be delicious. Mikus, however, had no problem telling me it was shit.

I curl up on the couch and flip through the TV guide. I circle *Knight Rider* after reading it's about a stolen car that leads Devon to a car show in Long Beach. I hope Jubal will be home to watch it with me.

The buzzer on the oven and the doorbell sound off at the same time. It startles me and for a split second I'm confused as to what I should do first, open the door or take the casserole out of the oven.

"Hi, Sawyer! Come in. I need to get dinner out of the oven. Lock the door behind you."

"Hi." Sawyer smiles and tosses his backpack onto the chair. He follows me into the kitchen. "It smells good in here."

"I hope it tastes good. Did you lock the door?" I fight the fear from my voice.

"Yeah. Why are you so concerned with the door? Should I be worried?"

"No. Just some of Mikus' cronies came by. They were almost as scary as Mikus."

I ask Sawyer if he'd rather sit at the table or in the living room. He opts for the table. I place the nicest pieces of Mikus' eclectic collection of dinnerware on the slightly wobbly table. The straight back green paisley chairs wobble slightly less.

"So, you graduated top of your class? I bet your parents are so proud of you." I smile.

"I do. And they are. My mom is planning a party. They are the ones who gave me the idea to come for a visit. I must talk about you a lot. They're excited to meet you."

This should make me happy, I know, but it only fills me with anxiety. I change the subject. "How's Jim? And Fancy?" I'm thankful he doesn't ask me to go to the party.

"Jim's fine. He sends his love. So does Fancy." Sawyer leans against the counter with his hands in his pockets. He looks so cute standing there I have to fight the urge to kiss him.

"I keep asking Jubal to take me back for a visit. I don't get to see him much lately. He's been working a lot in Reno. He promises he's going to take me to get my license but I've been waiting for three weeks."

We talk about Jim and Fancy and he tells me more about his family. I do not offer stories of mine.

"Ricky fell in the barn a couple weeks ago. He bruised some ribs and he has a concussion. I've been helping as much as I can. Marcus jokes that he's just trying to get out of working."

I excuse myself to the restroom after asking him to find a movie to watch. "Most of Mikus' movies are stupid but you might get lucky and find something good."

When I join Sawyer in the living room again, I see he has picked out two movies and wants me to choose. One of the movies is an old Western of Jubal's and the other is *It Happened To Jane*. "Are you serious?"

"What?" Sawyer smiles at me.

"Doris Day. Doris Day is my favorite actress. I can't believe you found that movie *here*."

"Actually, I brought this one. You told me on the lake that you love Doris Day movies and how she makes you happy, even on your worst days. I wanted to give you something that makes you happy. I'm not sure I get why you like old movies, though." He scrunches his nose.

69

I want to say thank you but instead I wrap my arms around his neck and kiss him. Why do I keep throwing myself on him? I'm pleasantly surprised to feel his arms close around me. He's not pulling away this time. He kisses me back. I feel like there are wild tigers in my chest and if I stop kissing Sawyer the animals will claw their way out of me.

My hands leave his neck and move down to his chest and abdomen. I lift his shirt to feel his skin and—the phone rings. It might as well have been a fire alarm or an explosion. We both jump away from the other and laugh nervously. I go into the kitchen to answer the phone.

"Hello? What do you mean? Jubal! We just finished eating and we're getting ready to start a movie. He brought a Doris Day movie. I know. Hey, I'm glad you called. After you left some guys showed up." Sawyer peaks his head in the kitchen to see if it's going well. My smile tells him we are in the clear. "Julio. Yes, that's what he said. Julio. I pretended like you were inside and they left. I came right inside and locked up. Sawyer is here now, so you can relax."

I hang up the phone and stand facing the wall because I'm too embarrassed to turn around. I know we can't go back to making out but that is the only thing I want to do.

"Ian, I think we should get to bed. We have to be up early or the fish will be full of bugs and we won't catch anything."

"I was thinking the same thing. We can watch the movie when we get back. I really think you'll like it. Jack Lemmon is a riot."

"That sounds like a plan. So, where am I sleeping? The couch?"

"Actually, there's a sleeper sofa in the room next to mine. I washed the sheets and dusted in there so it should be comfortable for you. I'll show you."

We shut off the lights and double check the locks before making our way upstairs. I flip on the light and let him walk past me. "Good night, Sawyer."

I brush my teeth and change into my pajamas. I crawl into bed feeling thankful I'm not alone in the house. I can't believe he remembered Doris Day. I lie there thinking of the people in my life. They follow me into sleep. Jubal takes me for my license. I fail the test. Sawyer tells me it's okay and I can try again. My father busts through the door and slaps me across the face. My mouth fills with the metallic taste of blood. He must've split my lip.

"Ian. Ian, it's okay. Wake up." Sawyer has me in his arms.

"Leave me alone. Don't you dare!" I'm struggling to get away from my father's grip but it's tight. I open my eyes and it's not my father holding me. It's Sawyer.

I sit up in my bed. I'm thankful Sawyer didn't turn on my bedroom light. I pray my embarrassment can't be seen by the dim glow coming in from the hallway. "I'm sorry, Sawyer."

"Don't be sorry. Are you okay?" Sawyer is still holding me.

"I'm okay. I'm sorry I woke you."

"I wasn't able to fall asleep. What were you dreaming about?"

"I don't remember," I lie. I just can't begin to explain that part of my life to him right now. "Will you stay with me?"

"Ian."

"I won't attack you. I promise." I lift the covers

and Sawyer slides in bed next to me. The warmth of his body relaxes me. I drift off almost instantly.

~~~~~~~~~

Sawyer is nudging me awake. I know it's time to go fishing but I don't want to move. "Noooo. I don't wanna get up."

"The fish aren't going to wait all day, Sleepy Head." Sawyer is on his side resting his head on his elbow. He brushes the hair from my face and softly kisses me.

"That's not gonna get me *out* of bed." I bury my head into his chest and hug him. I'm just not ready to let him go. The fish will be safe another day. Sawyer gives up and pulls the covers back around us and we fall asleep in each other's arms.

"What the hell is goin' on?" Jubal is standing in the doorway. He's surprised, but not angry—he *knows* Sawyer. He knows he's good and wouldn't take advantage of his hospitality.

I sit up and laugh but Sawyer is standing up and walking past Jubal. "Morning, Jubal. She had a rough night." He crosses the hall and shuts himself in the bathroom.

"Are you okay? Did Julio come back? What happened?" Jubal is sitting on my bed checking for signs of anything physically wrong.

"I'm okay now. I had another nightmare. Sawyer is amazing." I lean in closer to Jubal. "We kissed last night. You actually called right in the middle of it!" I punch his leg.

"Girl, why do you feel the need to tell me everything you're feeling or thinking or doing?"

"Because, Jubal. You're my best friend. You took

me in when you knew I was crazy. I love you for that." I reach around his big shoulders and hug him tight. I'm glad he's home.

"I left Mikus in Reno. We got into it. I'll explain later. I'm so hungry right now. You should make me some of them banana waffles. And maybe some eggs and potatoes." Jubal jumps up and heads out the door. Before leaving my room, he turns around. "I love you, too."

Chapter Eight

Jubal devours breakfast and insists we go fishing. Sawyer sits shotgun and I am in the backseat behind Jubal. He catches me staring at Sawyer in the rearview mirror. The first time he says nothing. The second time he shakes his head and laughs hard from deep in his belly.

"What's so funny?" Sawyer asks as he looks at Jubal then at me with a questioning look.

"Nothing!" I answer and slap Jubal hard on the arm.

"Easy, Killer!" Jubal wipes his eyes with his large hand and continues driving to the river.

Four hours pass and we have two fish. I've caught them both. "Can you feed us with these?" I ask Jubal as I hold up the stringer.

"It's your fault! Staying in bed all damn day!" Jubal lifts the lid on the cooler with one hand and points at me and Sawyer with the other.

I feel my cheeks blush. I'm not embarrassed that Jubal caught us. I'm embarrassed because I'd give anything to be in bed with Sawyer again. I feel like it's written on my forehead. I pray that there is not a line of drool running down my chin. I place my pole in the back and climb into the Blazer.

"Are you crashing at the house again, Sawyer?" Jubal glances back at me with his mischievous grin.

"I wasn't planning on it, but we did get a late start." It's Sawyer's turn to blush now.

We pull up next to the shed to unload the fishing gear. I'm relieved Mikus hasn't made it home from Reno, and I secretly wish his motorcycle breaks down and coyotes get him. I hope he doesn't show up before dinner. I'm looking forward to spending the evening with my two favorite people.

"What can I help with?" I ask as I climb out of the back seat.

"You can sit back and relax. We got this. Right, Sawyer?"

"You know it! We're gonna show you how men do up fish!" Sawyer flexes his muscles for added effect. It works. I'm lost in laughter.

I go inside and decide to shower the stench of fish off me. The shower is relaxing. I picture Sawyer's sweet smile and find I can't wait to get out of the shower to be with him again. I'm happy he's not leaving until morning. I brush out my hair and head to the kitchen.

"You smell great, Ian," Sawyer whispers to me as he pulls me in for a hug.

"So does dinner." I glance at the table and notice the fish has been fried and there are some potatoes and greens to go with it.

"I hope you don't plan on eating like you're used to," Jubal says, and laughs as he opens a beer.

The conversation over dinner starts out fun and playful until mention of Mikus. "You said you'd tell me later."

"I don't wanna talk about him right now. Let me enjoy the rest of my food."

Sawyer excuses himself to use the restroom. I look at Jubal and try again. "Can you tell me now?"

"Don't mention our business in front of Sawyer again. He don't need to get mixed up in our shit. I'm still scratching my head why your ass is still sittin' here."

His words aren't in anger. I can see the hurt in his eyes when he talks to me about this lifestyle. On our drives he tells me his dreams of the garage and how I'll be the shop manager. He's never been good with numbers. He's all the about the grunt work, he says. He hates dealing and promises to do anything to keep me out of it.

"Dinner was good but I really need some dessert. Who wants to run into town for ice cream?" Sawyer rubs his belly.

"You two go. I'll clean up here. Get me some Rocky Road. It's my favorite."

Sawyer holds my hand to his side of the truck and kisses me before opening the door. I climb in and crawl over to the passenger seat. I must look like an idiot with the enormous smile I have on my face. I try to tone it down a bit.

"Thank you for today, Ian. I've missed spending time with you. And Jubal."

"I'm so happy you came. I wish you didn't have to leave." Inside I know he can't stay. I don't want him to. Jubal is right. Our lives are messed up right now. Things will be better when he gets his shop.

Sawyer pushes in the cassette and REO Speedwagon's *Take It On The Run* plays through the speakers.

"I love this song."

"Me too. Maybe we can get tickets to see them in Sacramento."

I slide over next to him and lean my head on his shoulder. "I love when you talk about us doing things like that. I hope one day we can."

Sawyer pulls the truck off to the side of the road and puts it in park. "What do you mean, you hope?"

"Are you kidding? We live three hours away from each other. You're nineteen and I'm almost seventeen. You're finishing college soon and I'm a high school dropout. I have no idea what my future holds."

"I know what's in my future. It's you." Sawyer lifts my chin and kisses me.

I pull away. I love every word that just came out of his mouth. "I am?"

"If you want to be."

I straddle Sawyer's lap and my butt hits the steering wheel, honking the horn. I'm too focused on kissing Sawyer to care. He just reaches down and pulls the lever, allowing the seat to slide back.

Our hands explore each other's bodies while my hips move slightly back and forth on Sawyer's lap. Sawyer breaks away with a deep breath. "Okay. I think we better get that ice cream."

"Seriously?"

"Listen, our first time is not going to be in the front of my pickup on the side of the road."

"Okay." I climb back into my seat and adjust my top.

Sawyer scoots the seat forward after tugging at the crotch of his jeans. "I'm gonna need a cold shower."

"Maybe you can hold the ice cream on your lap!" I pull my hair up into a ponytail and try not to focus on his jeans.

We walk through the store until we find the ice cream aisle. Sawyer picks out Chocolate Mint and I grab a carton of Rocky Road for Jubal. It's a dark trip home. There is only a sliver of a moon out, but the stars are amazing. I point to the Big Dipper and Orion's Belt. They are the only two I know.

My heart sinks when I see Mikus' bike in the driveway. So much for my relaxing evening. When we park Jubal meets us at the porch. He hands me my backpack. The look on his face scares me. He's pissed off.

"Sawyer, I need you to take Ian to Jim's. I'll be there as soon as I can … I promise." He directs the last sentence to me.

I open my mouth to refuse but the crashing sounds coming from inside stop me. Jubal raises his hands to me. "Please. I'll see you soon, Ian." He turns and shuts the door behind him.

I'm standing there trying to figure out what just happened when I hear Mikus hollering from inside. I take a step towards the house. Sawyer takes my hand and leads me toward the truck. My eyes are unable to hold back the tears. I know he said he'd come for me but I feel like I've just been abandoned.

Sawyer is quiet. He hands me a tissue then pats the seat next to him. I move next to him and his hand rests on my thigh. I cry off and on the entire three hours to Jim's house, wondering what the hell is going on back at Mikus'.

Jim's lights are on. It's after midnight, so I know he's expecting us. I'm not sure if this is a good sign or not. I look at Sawyer, who gives me a small smile.

"Come on in," Jim hollers from inside the house.

We find him in the kitchen. He's pouring tea. He hands us each a cup and sits at the table. "Thank you, Sawyer, for getting her here. Will you be staying the night? I can make up a room for you."

"Thanks, Jim. But I better get home."

I walk Sawyer to the door where he gives me a long hug before kissing my forehead. I want to beg him to stay but I know it's best if he goes home. "Thank you for bringing me here."

"Try to get some sleep."

I go back to the kitchen. Jim sits sipping his tea. His jaw is tight. I have a million questions but know I must ask wisely because Jim can be a man of very few words. "What in the hell is going on?" *Very smooth, Ian.*

"All I know is Mikus got in some trouble. He's pissed off at Jubal for leaving him in Reno. I didn't get the details of what happened but he said it was all about money. He has to figure some shit out." He slams his hand on the table in anger.

"Jubal had to help Mikus out a while back. He needed a huge chunk of his savings to do it."

"Son-of-a-bitch!" Jim slams the table again. "That man can be dumb as shit sometimes!"

"Well, nobody can tell him any different. He's stubborn. I tried to question him and he bit my head off."

"It's late, Ian. Let's get to bed and hope to see Jubal tomorrow."

"Good night, Jim," I say sleepily.

~~~~~~~~

"Good mornin', Miss Ian. How've you been?" Marcus greets me with his warm Southern drawl as I walk into the kitchen.

"Hey, Marcus!" I hug him around his wide shoulders. "How's Ricky doin'?"

"He'll be in here in a few. He's slow to get goin'. I've 'bout had it with him." Marcus' words do not hide the fact that he's served up a plate of breakfast for his buddy.

I pile food high on my plate. I know how to cook but nothing tastes better than Jim's cooking. He said the next time I come for a visit he'd put a pig in the ground. I make a mental note to remind him of this.

"Ian." I turn to see Jubal standing in the doorway with Jim behind him. Jim has a smile on his face. I think he's as relieved to see Jubal as I am.

I jump up and sprint to Jubal. I stop in mid-run

when I see a bandage on his forearm. "What happened?"

"It's nothing. Come on. I need to talk to you." Jubal waves me to the door.

"I don't think so. Eat first. Then you can talk." Jim stands with his arms crossed in the doorway.

I make a plate for Jubal and say hi to Ricky, who's just walked in. He smiles and gingerly waves hello to us.

I offer to do the dishes but Jim says he'll take care of it. Jubal nudges my arm and nods to the door. I take my coffee with us to the back porch. I try to read his face but I'm unable to.

"I'm going to tell you something and I don't want you to interrupt. You can talk when I'm finished. Okay?" I nod my answer.

"Mikus is in some trouble. He owes that guy that came by the house a lot of money. A lot more money than I got in my savings. Mikus has no choice but to work off his debt. That means there's gonna be some changes. I promised you I'd never turn my back on you. You are my family now. But, so is Mikus. I can't turn my back on him either." Jubal takes a deep breath and leans against the railing.

"What are you trying to say, Jubal? Don't give me some bullshit story. If you are trying to tell me I have to leave, just say it." I sip my coffee from a shaking mug.

"Damn, girl. I said don't interrupt. I'm trying to tell you that Mikus is gonna be runnin' more coke. A lot more." Jubal rubs his head in frustration. "The problem is, he likes to do as much as he sells. And, he's an asshole when he's comin' down."

"Why don't we just leave? We can move into the house behind the garage. Jim told me he owns it. You don't have to…"

"Didn't you hear me? I said—I can't turn my back on him. He's messed up right now. He needs me. I've talked to Jim. He says you can stay here at the farm. If you want to."

His words punch me hard in the gut. "You talked to Jim?"

"Yes. I wanted to give you the option. It's your decision. I'm gonna go get more coffee. You think about it and let me know."

Jubal walks inside and I'm left sitting here confused as ever. This place is amazing. Jim's here... and Sawyer is here. But Jubal is my home now. Like he said, we're family.

Chapter Nine

"Don't be sad." Jubal glances at me from the driver's seat. "Jim promised he'd have Sawyer call."

"I just don't see why we couldn't stay. Jim was going to make us a pig. I wanted to see Sawyer." I stare out the window not wanting meet his eyes. I know I'm being childish but I am not ready to go back to Cavern Creek.

"You made your decision. I don't have time to sit around and shoot the shit with Jim and the guys. I have to work. I have to get my money back."

Now I'm flooded with guilt and anger. I close my eyes and try to sleep. It doesn't work. I'm too pissed off. "That's bullshit. You don't owe Mikus a frickin' thing! Family is family, you say. But Jim is family. I'm family!"

"It's not like that," Jubal says without looking at me.

"Then what's it like?" I refuse to let this go.

"You wanna know? All right, I was never into drugs when I was a kid. I got hooked on cocaine on the inside. When I got out, I needed it. I needed that high. Mikus took me in and tried to clean me up. He eventually did. But before he was able to, I burned him. I took anything I thought I could sell for my next high." Jubal grips the steering wheel and tears begin to sting his eyes. "He never turned his back on me. Not when I sold his record collection. Not when I sold his grandmother's locket thing."

"You never told me that. So, how did he turn from an upstanding guy to a drug dealing asshole?" My hatred for Mikus cannot be masked.

"I never said he was an upstanding guy." Jubal laughs. "But, he saw me at my worst and never gave up on me. He locked me in that room and took care of me through the retching, sweating, screaming and ugliness of withdrawals."

I think about my parents. They gave me life. They gave me food, albeit, not the healthiest food pyramid. They took care of me. But they also beat me until I spit up blood. They treated me like shit and if I hadn't made the decision to save myself, I'd probably be dead.

I will never look at Mikus and see anything but a slimy little redheaded worm.

"Want a milkshake?" Jubal points to the bright yellow arches on the right side of the highway.

"I'm sorry, Jubal." I am sorry. I'm sorry Jubal can't see there comes a point when you have to do what's best for you and break away from the poison in your life.

"I'm sorry, too. I just expect you to roll with all this crazy shit without explanation."

The girl in the drive-thru window hands Jubal his change and gives me a smile that shows off her braces. She reminds me of Janica Miller, with the kind of smile that masks her inner asshole. I'm in no mood to return her fake kindness. I just roll my eyes and poke the straw into the lid. Jubal cracks up laughing as he takes a long suck of strawberry shake.

"What's your problem?" Jubal looks at me with a crooked smile. "Too cute? Too nice?"

"Shut up. Girls like that piss me off. So fake. They just smile their bright smile and when you think maybe there's a friend behind the pearly whites, they pants you in the cafeteria."

Jubal chokes on his soda. "Now, the juicy stories come out. Did you kick her ass?"

"No. I wasn't embarrassed because the majority of the Seventh Grade saw my thankfully clean undies. I was scared that the teachers would see the bruises on my legs."

Jubal is no longer laughing or enjoying the story. "You are the strongest person I know. You had no idea what you'd find when you left home, but you went for it anyway."

"I knew it couldn't be any worse. I still have a little over a year until I'm truly free."

"That's right. Your birthday is in a few days."

"I don't expect anything, so don't feel like you need to make a big deal of it."

"I wasn't planning on it!" We both laugh.

~~~~~~~~~

Mikus sits quietly in the kitchen. He has bruises and cuts on his face and arms. I don't feel sorry for him. By the look of broken furniture and dishes, I can see how Jubal injured his arm. Mikus refuses to make eye contact with me.

"Man, you couldn't clean up?" Jubal pushes a chair out of his way and reaches in the fridge for a beer.

"I'm gonna put my stuff in my room." I return with a bottle of peroxide, band-aids and paper towels. Mikus looks at the bottle and finally meets my gaze.

"What the hell is that for?" Mikus tries to back away from my hand. I don't try to hide the pleasure this gives me.

"I can't do anything about the bruises, but I can try to prevent infection in these cuts. Don't be a baby."

Jubal laughs when Mikus winces at the slightest touch of the bubbling peroxide. "Yeah, don't be a baby, Mikus."

"Screw you, dude." Mikus gets the words out followed by a rant of cuss words brought on by pain.

"This one is pretty deep, Mikus. You probably need stitches."

"I'm not going to the ER. Can you do it?" Mikus looks up at me through blackened swollen eyes. I wonder who had the pleasure of causing his injuries.

"No. I can't stitch your face." I roll my eyes. "Jubal, do you have a First-Aid kit?"

Jubal nods and goes out to the garage. He returns with a red bag. I rifle through the bandages and gauze until I find the butterfly bandages. I do my best to fix him up. I hand him a fresh beer and start to clean up the mess.

Mikus looks at Jubal and then to me. "Thanks."

"Don't mention it. Now get out of here so I can clean up this mess. Does the rest of the house look like this?" I reach under the sink for a couple of garbage bags.

"Not really. Most of his meltdown took place in here." Jubal laughs.

"Screw you! You weren't the one gettin' your ass kicked by Julio and his band of thugs."

I get the mess cleared out of the kitchen and make my way to the living room. I stop when I overhear the two of them in a heated discussion. I move closer to the doorway to see if I can make out what they are saying.

"I don't know how you're gonna move so much. What were you thinkin'? Gambling? Really?" Jubal takes a long chug of his beer.

"Don't start on me again. I think I've learned my lesson."

"I just want my money back. I don't want to be in the middle of your mess."

"I remember a time when it was your mess, Jubal."

I grab two fresh beers and join them in the living room. "Here ya go." I sit in the corner of the couch and wait for them to continue their conversation.

"When do you plan on picking it up?" Jubal asks

without looking at him.

"I'll leave just after midnight. I figure a week in Reno should be enough."

I smile at the thought of having Jubal alone on my birthday. I think I'll ask if we can go fishing. I doze off thinking about a life without Mikus.

~~~~~~~~

"Hey. Wake up." Mikus kicks the cushion under my butt and I jerk awake.

"Where's Jubal?"

"He went into town for some more beer. You're not scared to be alone, are you?" Mikus stands over me with his beady eyes squinted in hatred for me.

"No. I'm not scared." I stand up on the cushion and sidestep around him. "Asshole."

"What was that?" Mikus grabs a handful of my hair and pulls me back to him. I don't let the pain show as he turns me to face him. "You stupid little girl. There's gonna be a time when Jubal won't be around to save you. Or better yet, he'll realize you're nothing but a liability and kick your ass back to the streets."

"Oh, Mikus." I tilt my head to the side. "That's all you got? Hair-pulling? No wonder you got your ass kicked." I reach up and grasp a handful of my own hair, pulling it out at the roots, and throw it at him.

"Shit! You are crazy." Mikus laughs an evil laugh.

Hearing Jubal's Blazer pull up to the house, we both call a truce to our who's-crazier-than-who game. Although I'm trembling inside, I will not back down from this piece of shit.

The three of us sit in the living room in silence. Jubal knows something went down but decides not to push the topic.

"Jubal, can you please take me for my license tomorrow?" I ask for the fourth time.

"Let me call Sheila and make sure she'll be there." Jubal leaves the room to make the call.

Mikus looks at me and I can feel the hate in his glare. I'm proud of myself for standing up to him but I feel guilty. Jubal doesn't need to be put in the middle. I do wonder who he'd pick if it comes down to it. Mikus must be wondering the same thing because when Jubal returns he looks back to the TV.

"Well, we can't test for a few days and we have to be there by eight before the other ladies get in." I jump up and hug him tight.

"Thank you, Jubal. I know you've taught me everything I need to know. I'll pass. I promise!"

"I better go pack. Good luck, Ian." Mikus fakes a smile.

"Thanks, Mikus. I'll be a licensed driver when you get home." I return the false friendship.

I'm waving them out the door when the phone rings. "Hello?"

"Hey, Ian. It's Sawyer."

"Hi, Sawyer! I'm sorry I didn't get to see you before we left." Just hearing his voice warms my body.

"Me too. I wanted to tell you my big news. My dad is going to Idaho to open a store. He's taking me with him."

"Sawyer, that's great! You were hoping he'd take you. I'm so happy for you. Call me when you get back, okay?" I hang up the phone and wonder what he sees in me, but I'm not interested in opening that can of worms so I push the thought from my head.

I say good night to Jubal and crawl into bed. I'm so excited to test for my license I find it impossible to sleep. I try to picture my future. The future Sawyer talks about. The garage is open and business is good. Sawyer is taking over the store as his father retires. Mikus, well, he's just not around. There's a ring on my finger. Our engagement picture in the paper doesn't worry me because I made it to my eighteenth birthday so my parents can't hurt me anymore. That is the thought that delivers me into sweet slumber.

Chapter Ten

"Congrats, girl! Let's go celebrate! Guess who's drivin'?" Jubal's smile is overflowing with excitement.

"I was so nervous. I thought I was going to fail. The lady took me through the school zone and I was going over the speed limit. I didn't realize it until she asked me how fast I was going."

"Well, you must've done everything else right," Jubal says as he hops into the passenger seat. "So, that was present number one. Are you ready for present number two?"

"I don't need anything else, Jubal. I told you not to make a big deal out of it."

"Well, I don't do much of what I'm told. Never have. Come on, Driver. Let's go home."

I'm expecting a present to unwrap but when I walk into the living room I'm face to face with Jim and Sawyer. The best surprise I could ever ask for. "How? Where's your truck?"

"Happy birthday! We parked behind the garage. I told you I wanted to make you a cake." He points to the coffee table, to a cake with "*Happy 17th, Ian*" in sloppy cursive writing.

I wrap my arms around his neck and kiss him square on the mouth. I don't care that Jubal and Jim are one step away from us. I hug Jim next. "I've never had such a perfect birthday."

"I wish we could stay longer, but you only have us for lunch," Jim explains. "I gotta get back to the farm and Mr. Sawyer here has a store to open in Boise."

"Well, we have more than a birthday to celebrate then." Jubal slaps Sawyer on the back.

"What would you like? I can make pork chops or chicken. I think we have some fresh corn in the fridge." I go to the fridge to look.

"Don't be silly, Ian. You're not going to cook for us on your birthday. We're taking you out." Sawyer takes my hand and moves me away from the fridge.

I run upstairs and throw on one of my new outfits Jubal got for me. I brush through my hair and try not to focus on my reflection. I really need a makeover.

I come downstairs to catch the end of a hushed conversation. The three of them stare at me in silence. I choose not to come down from Cloud Nine, so I say nothing.

"Let's get going. I'm starving." Jubal leads the way.

I'm the last out of the door. The guys part in front of me. "Happy birthday!" They sing in unison. They hold their arms out like the models on *The Price Is Right* showcasing a car.

It's not a new car. It's actually on the ugly side, as far as paint goes. But according to them, it's mine. "Are you serious? It's amazing!"

"Don't worry about the color, that's just primer. It's a solid car. Of course, you can only drive locally. No trips into Nevada. It's too risky."

"Thank you." Those are the only words I can get out. Tears flow down my cheeks as I hug each one.

"Well, hop in. Let's see how she rides." Jim hands me the keys.

It takes me a couple of minutes to get my breathing under control and my eyes clear enough to see the street signs. The interior is clean. I'm thankful it's an automatic. I turn the ignition with trembling hands. I'm in love.

"I can't stop smiling. You guys are sneaky."

"Well, the bike in the garage was more of a

project to keep you busy, but we wanted you to have a car. I'll sleep better, that's for sure." Jubal laughs his fabulous laugh.

I park at the diner and flashback to the first time Jubal and I ate here. "Jubal, do you remember our first meal here?"

"How can I forget? You called me a pimp!"

"You're going to have tell us *all* about it," Sawyer says as he climbs out of the back seat.

I spend my birthday with three of the greatest men on the planet. I couldn't ask for anything more. We share funny stories and enjoy delicious food. I don't want it to end. But it does. Before I know it we are on the way back to the house.

"I'll make some coffee for your trip back home." Jubal puts his hand on his brother's shoulder and they disappear inside.

Sawyer spins me around and kisses me like he's been holding back as long as possible. I reciprocate. I love the way Sawyer makes me feel and I cannot wait to be in Mission Valley with him for good.

"I have a little something for you." Sawyer moves to place something in my hand. "Don't get too excited though."

"Too late! I'm super excited!" I kiss him. "Sawyer! It's a ring."

"It's my class ring. I want you to wear it. Here's the chain." Sawyer pulls out a small box from his pocket.

"I love it. Thank you, Sawyer. Does this mean I'm your girlfriend?"

"That's what I'm hoping for. Turn around so I can put it on."

I move my hair out of his way so he can clasp the necklace. I can feel his hands shaking. I wonder how he can be nervous. He's so hot and smart and funny. There must be something wrong with him if he's interested in me.

Saying goodbye to them is harder this time. I miss them so much. I just want to hold onto them and keep them forever. I've never had so many people care about me. It's a terrific feeling. I wave until they are out of sight. I spend the rest of the evening looking at the ring.

Jubal wakes with a great idea to get my mind off of the guys. He's making me take off the tires and put them back on. He's also having me check all the fluids. "I gotta know you can take care of yourself if you get stuck on the side of the road."

We turn at the sound of Mikus' bike. He's not alone. He has three other guys with him.

"Get to your room. I'll be up in a few." Jubal wipes his hands with a rag and walks towards Mikus.

I make a mad dash inside, stopping at the fridge for a soda. The window in my room faces the back of the house so I am blocked from view of the garage. I turn the radio on to Dr. Love who is in the middle of a heated discussion about what to do about a cheating spouse. I'm a firm believer in second chances but this guy has screwed more women than Wilt Chamberlain. "Dump him."

I wake to a darkened room. Shouting reverberates off the walls. I'm confused. I don't have a clue what time it is or who is yelling. I flip on the light and clumsily find my slippers. I'm still rubbing my eyes when I get to the source of the commotion.

"How dare you! How messed up are you, man? You bring your thug buddies here to host a blow party? You're supposed to be selling the shit, not snorting it." Jubal has his hands clenched in anger.

The living room light is dancing on the sweat on Jubal's arms making his muscles look even larger than usual.

"Yes, I did. I invited *my* friends to *my* house. If you don't like it, tough shit." Mikus' blue eyes are almost completely black. He's wired and feeling invincible.

Jubal notices me standing there. He releases his clenched fists and his body relaxes with a deep sigh. "You're wrong, Mikus. They're not your friends." He points to me and motions me to go back to my room. "Ian, go get your shit. We're out of here."

These words suck every bit of high from Mikus' being. He stands in front of Jubal begging him to change his mind. "Come on, man. I didn't mean it. Don't be like this. I won't do the shit anymore."

"It's too late. I appreciate all you've done for me. But, I can't live like this anymore. I don't want Ian to live this way either." Jubal looks and frowns when he realizes I'm still frozen to the spot.

"You've gone soft since that little girl showed up. You've changed." Mikus looks at me with disgust.

"I just want a good life. That doesn't make me soft." He turns from Mikus and guides me into the hallway.

"It'll be a real shame for her to get sent back to Mommy and Daddy!" Mikus hollers after us.

I stop dead in my tracks. My heart is suddenly beating so loud I can't hear anything else. Jubal is pulling me off Mikus. He easily picks me up but that doesn't stop me from trying to land another punch to Mikus' face.

"Get that crazy bitch away from me! Sure makes it easy to make the call, though." Mikus rubs his suddenly swelling cheekbone.

"Don't be like that, man."

"I can't have you leave. We're partners."

"We're not staying." Jubal takes two steps down the hall.

"Wait!" My mind is racing from what's just happened. "We'll stay. I'll help you get out of trouble with Julio. I'll drop for you. Just don't call." I still have a year before I'm free.

"What the hell are you doing?" Jubal has a tight grip on my arms.

"He'll do it, Jubal. He'll turn me in. I can't go back!"

Suddenly, Mikus has found his high again. He smiles at me then looks to Jubal. "What do ya say, Jubal? We back in business?"

Jubal says nothing. He releases my arms and walks to his room, slamming his door behind him.

I don't have to turn around to know Mikus is right behind me. I can feel his breath on my neck. I take one step out of the living room and hear his snaky voice behind me. It's almost a whisper. "You'll pay for that." I just keep walking.

"Jubal? Can I come in?" Jubal opens his door in reply.

"What were you thinking? I'm trying to do the right thing for once in my life and you just signed up for some shit you ain't ready for."

"I had no choice."

"He wouldn't have called."

"Yes! He would have! I saw it in his eyes, Jubal."

"Just go to bed."

"Don't be mad at me."

"I'm not! Just go. Please." Jubal's shoulders drop in defeat.

I shut and lock my bedroom door. It is now I feel

the weight of what I've done. Maybe I should run away again—I cause so much trouble. This realization brings on tears I cannot control. I crawl into bed and, as quietly as possible, cry myself to sleep.

Chapter Eleven

"Come on, already! We've gone over this a million times. I know the drill."

"You stupid little girl. You think this is fun for me? You have to know what the hell you're talking about or they'll take more than they pay for or worse, they'll think you're a narc." Mikus is working on his fourth beer in the last hour.

"Don't be a jerk. I think she's got it."

"You'd think so. It's been three months. If she sells a gram for forty bucks, it's comin' out of your asses." Mikus reaches into the fridge for his fifth Budweiser.

"There's one last thing. We need to get you some clothes and a haircut." Jubal tosses me the keys and we leave Mikus at the table.

"Get more beer while you're out!" Mikus calls after us.

I convince Jubal to get a bite before the "makeover". He chats with Betty at the counter while I step into the restroom. When I return to the table, I find Jubal has ordered the food I like and there is a Coke with no ice waiting for me. He knows me.

"Why do I have to change the way I look? I mean, what's wrong with the way I look?" I twist the wrapper from my straw around my fingers until it breaks.

"You look fine the way you are. It's just… safer. You have to look like a little innocent girl walking through the casinos looking for her family."

He has a point. I look like I could pass for a homeless person. I guess I'll look for clothes that Lucy Wells would buy. She was every teacher's pet. She was nice to every person she saw. Even me.

"Finish up. It's time for your haircut. Did you

decide on a style?" Jubal counts out bills to cover lunch and leave a decent tip for Betty while he waits for me to finish the last of my fries.

"I think I'll just trim it. I don't need to change it, just style it. I can change the style more if I keep it long. I can't wait to get some ugly goody-two-shoes clothes! I'm not kidding. I hope you brought a ton of cash to pay for all of the outfits I'm going to get."

The sun is warm and the slightest breeze makes this day almost perfect. I miss Sawyer. I haven't talked to him much. I almost walk into a light pole, but Jubal jerks me out of the way at the last second.

"What are you doin'?" Jubal is laughing his deep full-bodied laugh.

"Oh, shut up!" I join in his laughing fit. I don't tell him I'm thinking about Sawyer. I'll never hear the end of it.

I'm bent over in laughter. When I stand my laughter catches in my throat. I can feel the blood drain from my face.

"What's wrong?" Jubal is looking from me to the empty street around us.

"Uh, nothing. I thought I saw someone."

"Who?"

"Nobody, I guess."

"Well, come on then."

My lunch is threatening to stain the black cape Lilly has just wrapped around me. "Honey, can I get you some water or something?" Her soft hands are cradling my chin.

"Yes, please." I look at Jubal, who is standing there speechless. "Jubal, I'm fine. I think lunch upset my stomach."

I sit in the chair while Lilly and Jubal visit. I try to

picture my mother's face. She was standing there watching me. I saw her pink sundress and short hair. I'm facing the mirror but my eyes are staring at the door, waiting for her to come in and haul me away. She doesn't come. Maybe it wasn't her. The lady standing there watching me was smiling. It couldn't have been her.

"All finished. What do ya think?" Lilly removes the cape and brushes stray hairs from my neck.

"I love it!" I don't say this just to be polite. I've never looked in the mirror and liked what I saw. I'm so shocked my hands cup my face just for a second. "The layers look so pretty!"

"I agree. How can a haircut make such a big difference?" Jubal is smiling at me.

"Well." Lilly explains. "All that hair has been hiding her beautiful face." Lilly points to the floor.

Jubal pays Lilly for the haircut and some styling products before we make our way to the second-hand store. I'm glancing around for the pink sundress but I'm beginning to think the jalapeños on my chili fries must've caused hallucinations. There is no lady even remotely resembling my mother anywhere.

I try on a ton of outfits. The clothes smell like moth balls and make me a bit sick to my stomach. We choose six outfits. Four are very lady-like and the other two are my normal tomboy style.

I glance over at the purses when I see the perfect backpack. "Look!"

"What?" Jubal jumps at my excitement.

The pack is purple with rainbows and stars. It's very bright and childish. "It's *amazing*, isn't it?" I throw it over my shoulder and model it. Jubal rolls his eyes.

I listen to Jubal sing his country songs as he drives us home. I find myself unable to stop playing with my hair. I wonder if Sawyer will like it.

"Better get to bed. We have a long couple of days in front of us," Mikus slurs. He hasn't slowed his alcohol consumption, even after laying down his bike last week because he was three sheets to the wind.

"I'll be fine." I roll my eyes and turn my attention to Jubal. "Good night, Jubal." I make sure to enunciate *Jubal* so Mikus knows I'm ignoring him. Childish, I know. But he's a dick.

Even in my sleep I can see the lady on the corner watching me. Her smile is beautiful. I don't know if I'm making up her smile in my head or if I actually saw the woman. I do know it was not my mother. My mother wouldn't have been smiling. She'd be disheveled and stumbling across the street to pull my ass back to my father's clutches.

~~~~~~~~~

"Get up. It's time to go. Jubal's already left." Mikus pulls the door closed behind him.

"Jubal left?" I'm still trying to wake up. I feel as if I just fell asleep. "Asshole." I figure he doesn't hear me but he's in my room leaning over me with his fist ready to unload a blow to my face.

"Listen, you little bitch. This is my house. You will show me respect." Mikus spits on my cheek as he separates each word in his demand.

"You won't hit me. A cute little innocent girl, walking through a casino with a big shiner, will stick out like crazy." I tilt my head and smirk at his now red face.

He slams the door again. I pull on the ugliest outfit we picked out. Even after two washes I can smell a hint of mothballs. The pastel pink slacks are comfortable but the sleeveless teddy bear sweater feels itchy on my skin. I do my best to recreate the hairstyle Lilly showed me. I put the tube of clear lip-gloss in my pocket.

I meet Mikus in the kitchen. He's eating a fried egg and washing it down with an ice-cold beer. Classy. "Why did Jubal leave? Is something wrong?"

"Sylvia needed him." Mikus doesn't look up from his food to answer me.

"Okay. I'll be in the car."

"We're going on my bike."

"I'm *not* riding on your bike with you, Mikus."

"You don't have a choice. Let's go." He tosses his dirty plate and silverware into the sink. "You can clean that up when we get back."

This is going to be a long ride. The thought of being so close to Mikus the asshole makes my skin crawl. I know Jubal wouldn't have left me unless he had to. I will let him know how displeased I am with the travel arrangements, though.

We park in front of a familiar looking bar: Sylvia's Place. A smile covers my face the second Jubal steps out onto the street.

"Hey. You made it. I'm sorry I had to bail. Sylvia's place was broken into. My guess is a couple of thug kids wanted to get drunk and play some pool. Although to listen to her tell it, the place will never recover."

I decide to forgive Jubal. The inside of the bar smells like a mixture of Pine Sol and vomit. I offer to help Sylvia clean up. She starts telling us how she found this place. By the end of it she's so fired up she snaps one of her two-inch-long fingernails off, and a curse-filled rant follows her into the back room.

I'm dressed in my horribly girly clothes with a childish backpack full of coke walking through Fitzgerald's Casino. I glance back to Jubal, who is ordering a drink at the bar. He gives me a *"You can do this"* look. I give him a grin and board the elevator.

I push the button for the twelfth floor and stare at the shoes of the other passengers. I remember everything Mikus told me. I give the guy his order but try to get him to buy more by telling him how pure this batch is.

I knock on room 1244. The hairiest man I've ever seen opens the door. I try to hide my shock but my eyes must be bulging from their sockets. He is standing in a robe that is barely tethered closed. I'm not sure where his chest hair ends and his facial hair begins. He holds the door wide and guides me inside. I draw a deep breath and take two steps.

"Don't be shy, darling. I won't bite. Unless you want me to." He laughs a gross laugh and walks over to the table next to the bed. He opens the drawer and I see a pistol and a wallet. I'm hoping he grabs the money and is not planning on robbing me. Mikus didn't prepare me for that. He clutches the wallet and the bathroom door opens behind me. I let out a squeal and turn to face a woman standing there with only a towel wrapped around her head.

"Hi. You're a cutie. What are you doing here?" Being naked in front of strangers does not bother her a bit. And I thought I was comfortable with my body. I try to focus on her eyes and not her large, I'm guessing fake, boobs.

"She has our party favors, darling. Should we ask her to stay?" He looks at me as he rubs his fingers through the curly hairs of his chest.

I feel like I might vomit. These people are obviously high already if they think I'm staying a second longer than I have to. "I actually have a lot of other parties to deliver to, but thanks."

I walk past the bar and toward the exit knowing Jubal will be following behind me. I still feel the urge to vomit. So much adrenaline pulsing through me is causing my legs to feel like rubber. I make it to the Blazer and lean against the bumper. Jubal unlocks the door and starts the engine. I climb into the passenger seat and once the door is open, I let out a combination of a laugh and a scream.

"It's pretty crazy, ain't it?" Jubal laughs.

I tell him about the hairy guy and the naked lady. I sold them two more grams than they ordered. I just wanted out of there. "Jubal, what do I do if I get into trouble?"

"What do you mean? If someone hurts you?"

"I wasn't worried about that. Those freaks wanted to keep me for the night!" Jubal finds this hilarious. I guess it is funny—now that I'm out of the situation.

Three more drops and we are on our way back home. I can do this. I'm having no trouble getting rid of the coke and the people think it's cute that a little girl is making the delivery. The lady at the second drop laughs and makes a joke that I'm delivering Girl Scout 'cokies'.

Mikus is pacing the kitchen when we walk in. He is in the best mood I've ever witnessed. He laughs and high fives us both, then tells us how he's had five calls since he's been home. "They are loving this!"

Suddenly, I'm his best friend. Jubal gives small grins now and then, but I can tell this makes him very nervous. I know how Mikus can be and I've known him a lot less time than Jubal. I don't care as long as we get Jubal's money. Then I'll drop Mikus like a bad habit.

"I'm gonna grill up some burgers. Ian, can you make your fabulous potato salad?" Mikus asks in a new cheery voice.

The phone rings when I'm cutting potatoes. I pick up the receiver expecting to hear from one of Mikus' drug buddies but it's Sawyer. Suddenly, I feel guilty for getting involved with Mikus. I try not to let it show in my voice.

"How's my girl?" Sawyer sounds tired. "I miss you so much."

"I miss you too, Sawyer. I can't wait to see you." I hold his class ring and move it back and forth on the chain.

"Well, I'm sorry to say it might be a while. I've been going back and forth to Idaho so much with this new location. The original buyers backed out causing all kinds of problems. I'm actually getting ready to head back in the morning. I just wanted to hear your voice."

My heart sinks. Sawyer is so amazing and honest. I am now a drug dealer. Or at least I'm a drug delivery girl—a mule. "I'm so glad you called. It seems like it's been forever since we've talked."

I sulk all through dinner and excuse myself to bed early. I just need to be alone. How will he react if he finds out? The thought of disappointing Sawyer makes me want to go tell Mikus to stuff it. But, I know we need to get his ass out of trouble so Jubal can get his shop. This is all Mikus' fault.

Chapter Twelve

I'm getting used to my schedule. Jubal has been working a lot of shifts at Sylvia's. I haven't heard from Sawyer in almost a month. Mikus is still being nice to me but the hate we share is returning to a normal level. It's usually after I unload a shipment that he's happy and only when he remembers I'm doing a better job at getting rid of the drugs than he did that his disgust for me returns.

Wednesdays mean doing as little as possible. The three of us laze around and enjoy some much-needed downtime. Jubal wants to play cards. I don't know how to play, but he offers to teach me. Mikus is in a foul mood but agrees to join us. Jubal can tell right away that Mikus is high.

"You said you were done, man."

"What are you talkin' about? I never said I was done with shit. I said I wouldn't do *all* of the blow." He laughs. "Julio won't know the difference. He's actually been pretty decent since Ian has come on board."

"You told him I was delivering?" Fear warms my face at the thought.

"No, you idiot. People talk. Word gets around. It's not like you have a name tag on."

"Screw you, Mikus! I'm so tired of saving your ass only to have you ruin everything."

Before I can duck, he connects an open hand to my cheek. I see stars. But I also see red. I take the fork from my TV dinner and stab it into Mikus' hand before Jubal can stop me. All three of us are screaming at each other, but Jubal wins. He's got Mikus by the collar with one hand and pushes me into the chair with the other.

"What the hell? Ain't you bored with this shit? I know I am." Jubal releases Mikus. "Go wash your hand. And if you lay a finger on her ever again, it'll be the last thing you ever do."

"*Seriously*? She stabbed me with a fucking fork and you're gonna take her side?" Mikus cowers his way out of the kitchen, mumbling the whole way.

I look at Jubal, who can't help but grin at me. "What?" I ask incredulously.

"You stabbed him with a fork!" Jubal tries to whisper. "I'm sorry that he hit you, but I don't think I have to worry much about you taking care of yourself anymore!"

"I didn't plan on stabbing him. I just went off. He really does ruin everything."

Jubal laughs and hands me a washcloth with ice to help with the swelling. "I don't think Mikus will be joining us for the rest of the night."

We put the cards away and watch a Western. I must fall asleep during it, because Jubal is nudging me awake. "Time to go to bed."

"Is the movie over?"

"Yep. You didn't miss much. It wasn't John's best work."

I say good night to Jubal and lock myself in my room. I crawl into bed and quickly fall back to sleep. Something wakes me up. I creep to the door and put my ear to it, hoping to identify the sound. It's the television. Jubal must not be able to sleep.

I step out into the hall and realize Jubal's door is closed. I tiptoe to the living room and see Mikus sitting on the couch getting a blowjob from some lady I've never seen before. I stop in my tracks but before I'm able to turn around he looks over at me and smiles, all the while flipping me off with his bandaged hand.

Jubal must sense the tension between me and Mikus because when I wake up he tells me to get my backpack. Since I left home, I always have a bag packed. Jubal tells me that's just smart thinking. You never know when you might have to run.

I climb into the Blazer and notice he's packed it full of camping gear. I see a tent, fishing poles, firewood, ice chests and a case of beer along with a case of Cragmont soda pop for me. "You're taking me *camping*?"

"You've been working hard and I'm afraid if I don't separate the two of you somebody's gonna get hurt again." Jubal starts up the engine and pulls down the long tree-lined driveway.

"It's not my fault. Well, not all my fault. He's such an asshole. We are so close to being out of here. I should just kill him with kindness. Or a knife." I say the last three words under my breath.

Jubal takes us into the mountains to a place God must've led him to. Who could've known that this beautiful place existed? There is a small lake sitting in the canyon surrounded by tall mountains covered in tall pine trees. The camp sites face the lake. Behind the lake is a large mountain that has suffered several rock-slides.

"We can set up camp and hike to the falls." Jubal has the back open and he's setting things where he's envisioning our camp.

I try to help Jubal by staying out of his way. He's moving with a purpose and I'm more of a hindrance than help. I crawl into the tent and unfold the cots and sleeping bags while he sets up his makeshift kitchen.

"What's up with the metal box?" I pop open a soda and sit in a chair by the fire pit.

"That is a bear box."

"Excuse me?"

"It's where we put the food so the bears don't get

it."

"Bears? Are you shitting me?"

"No. We're in the woods. Where bears live."

"And we are sleeping in a canvas house! Won't the bears just eat *us*?" I'm pretty sure I'm scaring all wildlife away with this rant. I know bears live in the woods. It never occurred to me that I'd ever be in close proximity to them.

"I've never seen you act like such a girly girl! This is great!" Jubal is staring at me with wide eyes and enjoying the panic in my face.

"Laugh it up. I'm sleeping in the Blazer."

Jubal grabs the poles and his tackle box then leads the way to the falls. "You can sleep wherever you want. The bears aren't going to get you."

"Not unless they break a window."

"It's been known to happen."

"Jubal!"

We come to a clearing of tall pines and I lose my breath. The sight in front of me is out of a dream. The water flows swiftly spilling over rocks and crashing into the bottom in white fluffy caps.

We toss our lines into the fresh water. Immediately my thoughts are of Sawyer. I miss him. I have no patience for fishing today. I set my pole on the beach and walk over to Jubal. In such a short amount of time he's caught two fish and is reeling in his third.

"Can we go visit Jim? I miss him. There is something so peaceful about Freedom Farms."

"We'll be leaving soon. For good."

"Are you serious? We get to leave?" I can't control myself. I wrap my arms around his neck.

We make our way back to camp where Jubal builds a fire and I season the fish. I'm thankful it was

Jubal who caught them because I hate cleaning fish. I slice a lemon and put chunks of butter in with the fish, then wrap them in foil packets. Jubal boils some water for my hot chocolate. He adds a little bit of peppermint schnapps to help with my nerves. It's delicious.

I sit mesmerized by the crackling fire. My fear of being eaten by a bear has melted in the fire pit along with the million thoughts battling inside my head. It's as though for every second I watch the dancing flames, a fear or stressor jumps into the fire where the wisps of smoke carry them up into the darkening sky.

Jubal has a similar glazed look on his face. The two of us sit in silence until dinner is ready. The fish smells amazing. I put on the thick leather fire glove to pull the potatoes from the fire, giving them a squeeze to make sure they are cooked.

I'm feeling the schnapps kick in along with a full stomach, and I'm ready for bed. Jubal lets me crawl in the tent and change before coming inside. The sleeping bags smell of campfire. It's strangely relaxing. Jubal turns the kerosene lamp off and suddenly I'm aware of the night sounds.

"Jubal. What's it like?"

"What's what like?"

"Getting high. What's the difference between smoking pot and doing coke?"

I don't realize it's such a loaded question until Jubal is sitting on the edge of his cot and the kerosene lamp is fired back up.

"What kind of question is that? Just how interested are you? You better not ever smoke a bowl or do a line. I mean ever!"

"Jubal! I'm just asking. I don't see how it has so much power over people. Mikus has changed so much.

His behavior. His looks. Were you like that?"

I notice Jubal's shoulders relax when he realizes I'm just curious.

"I was worse. I lied, cheated, and stole. I only had eyes for the drug. I overdosed twice. I never felt happy that I lived until I met your crazy ass."

"We found each other for a reason."

"You think so, Ian?"

"I do. We were both sad for too long. Now we are each other's happy."

"When you talk this way all I feel is guilty."

"Why do you feel guilty? You saved me from a life on the streets."

"I put a roof over your head is all. You're living the same lifestyle as the streets. That's my fault." Jubal turns the lamp off and we lie in the darkness.

"We'll be out of it soon." My eyelids are growing heavy. "You'll have Jubal's Garage and I'll have Sawyer."

"About the garage… I've changed the name. It's gonna be JV's." Jubal's words make their way to my ears but I am too sleepy to respond.

I awaken to the delicious smell of breakfast. I throw on some fresh clothes before unzipping the tent. "Did you mean…?"

"Hey, Ian." A freshly bruised Mikus is sitting by the fire stirring the coals with a stick he's just finished whittling.

"Where's Jubal?" My pulse thumps out of beat. I stare down at the hole in my shoe so Mikus can't see the red in my cheeks.

"He's down by the lake."

"How'd you know where we'd be?"

"Shit. We've been camping here for years."

Mikus smiles, causing the split in his lip to bleed again.

I don't ask him what happened. I honestly don't care. I just keep looking for Jubal. Mikus doesn't have his normal bite to him. He must be very hurt. I want to high-five the guy who did it to him.

"Did Jubal tell you the good news? He's got enough for the garage." I look at him for a reaction but he only gives a small grin.

"Don't pack just yet, little girl."

I want to grab the cast iron skillet from the fire and smack him in his stupid face. How can just a tiny smug grin piss me off so badly? He's a lowlife druggie that hates me for simply being alive. *That's it*—he reminds me of my father.

"Well, look who's up. Let's eat so we can hike to the top of the falls. It's awesome up there. You thought it was beautiful at the bottom. It's even better from the top. You'll love it." Jubal stands there holding the dishes he's just rinsed in the lake.

The three of us sit by the fire. The guys are shoveling food in but I've lost my appetite. I sip hot chocolate, making a point to stare at Jubal the entire time. I don't know what I missed this morning but I can't wait to find out.

Jubal leads the way and as soon as we are out of earshot he turns on me. "I need you to shut your mouth. You listen to every word I say. Mikus is clean. Well, he's getting clean. He pissed Julio off again and needs our help. One more month. That'll get us out and get Mikus off the hook. He gave me his word. You can go to Jim's if you'd rather."

"Why do you keep trying to pawn me off on Jim? I'm not going anywhere. You do realize this *one last time* bit is getting old. He's not going to get clean." I walk ahead of Jubal back towards camp, not wanting to hear another word. I pull a branch from a nearby bush and angrily pull the leaves and toss them to the ground. "I don't want to see the falls."

I crawl into the tent, hastily zipping myself inside. I regret it instantly. It has to be one hundred degrees. Beads of sweat form on my face immediately. It takes less than five minutes for me to exit the sauna. Jubal gives me a small grin and hands me a soda. I plop into a chair I drag into the shade. Defeated, I drag my finger along the red and white braided nylon straps beneath me.

"Ian? I want to let you know I'm sorry. I messed up good this time. Jubal told me you've agreed to stay for a little bit longer. I'm going to ride straight from here on out." Mikus crushes a Budweiser can and pops open another.

"Forgive me if I think you're full of shit. I've heard it before. Jubal might fall for it, but I know better. I'm staying for Jubal. Not you. And I *am* going to stay a few days with Jim. I need to see him. I need to see Sawyer." I don't look at him when I speak. I just continue to focus on the pattern of my chair.

Jubal asks me to help him pack up camp. Mikus chugs one more beer before heading home on his bike. We finish loading the Blazer and douse the fire before leaving. We drive for a while in silence. I don't mind. I stare out the window at the beautiful scenery.

"We'll give him one more month. Okay? I promise."

Chapter Thirteen

"There's our girl!" Jim stands to greet me on his porch steps. Fancy is by my side carrying her 'baby' with her tail wagging in excitement.

I hug Jim for a very long time. I'm so tired. I want to share with him everything I've been up to. My words are close to spilling from my mouth when the screen door opens and I see Sawyer standing there looking as handsome as ever. My breath catches in my chest. I take in the sight of him and lock it away in my mind.

"I've missed you! Come here." Sawyer holds his arms out and envelops me in the tightest squeeze I can handle. I don't move, wanting to stay in his arms forever. Suddenly, I feel that familiar feeling of guilt and shame.

"Jim has been cooking for you all day. He's made your favorite. Actually, I think he's made everyone's favorite!" Sawyer takes my bag and leads me inside.

It feels so amazing being here in Jim's kitchen. We share stories and catch up. Sawyer has been a huge help to his father. The store in Idaho has really taken off. His next project is in Montana. I'm so proud of him. Jim asks if I've been studying for my GED. I tell him I have, and it's not a complete lie. I do have the study guide he found for me. I've even opened it a couple of times.

Jim shows me Fancy's litter. They are beautiful, little bundles of fur tripping over each other. I am immediately in love with the runt of the litter.

"Do they have names?"

"No. I can't even tell them apart yet. Do you have a name in mind?" He pets the little runt I now have in my arms.

"Yes. I think I'll name her Calamity Jane. You know, Doris Day played her. She was small but fearless. Of course, I'll call her CJ."

"That's a great name. I think you should've been named CJ." Sawyer stands behind me and wraps his arms around my waist. My tummy is filled with butterflies.

Sawyer asks me to take a walk with him. "There's a full moon tonight. Go on, enjoy it," Jim says as he takes our empty dishes.

The soft breeze gives life to the shadows of the trees, the moon illuminating the graveled road. Walking hand in hand, Sawyer tells me the manager of the Idaho location was a total tool. "He treated me like I was a twelve-year-old. I had to set him straight. I did the whole *I may be young, but I'm not an idiot* spiel. It was ridiculous. I'm going to have to get used to it until I no longer look like a youngster. I've worked so hard to finish school early, as well as college."

"I bet it felt great to put him in his place. I'm so proud of you, Sawyer. You make me want to be a better person." I let go of his hand and pick up a handful of gravel. I suddenly feel nervous.

"What do you mean? You're a terrific person. You're my girl." Sawyer pulls me in and kisses me. It's a soft kiss. It's a kiss that tells me he means what he says.

"Sawyer. I've done things that I'm not proud of." I can't believe I'm spilling my guts. He's going to run for the hills.

"What things? Are you married? Are you working at the Mustang Ranch?" Sawyer laughs.

"No! Jeez. I'm just a runaway punk girl." I can't do it. I can't have him not see me as he does now. He'll see me differently if he knows I'm a drug dealer and a liar.

"You always think so little of yourself. I don't get it. You are brave and smart. And funny. When I'm on the road and missing home, I think of you. I picture your beautiful face and that smile." He brushes his fingers along my bottom lip. "Yes … that smile."

We get back to the house and sit on the swing. Hours pass, but we don't run out of things to talk about. He is fascinating to me. To accomplish so much at twenty is amazing. It was nice to talk about finance and business law. I excelled in school, but running away put a halt to my education. I still read. Jubal gets me library books. I've read several vehicle manuals. Talking with Sawyer awakens a part of me that lies dormant in my daily life.

"I'm super tired. Will you come by tomorrow?" I want to ask him to sneak up to my room, but control the urge to ask.

"Actually, I want you to come meet my parents tomorrow. I know you've met my dad at the store, but I'd really like to take you home to *meet my parents.*"

I'm not sure how one word can cause instant panic, shaking, sweats and uncontrollable fidgeting. *Parents.* Sawyer must sense my tension, because he stands and pulls me into his arms.

"I will never do anything to hurt you. I will never let anyone hurt you. I've already explained to them about your parents and they won't be bugging you about it. I promise."

He leans in to kiss me and I'm so touched by his kindness I pull him closer to me, kissing him with a growing passion. My skin is tingling. I never want to stop kissing him.

"I can't wait until I'm here with you for good. You make me feel so happy. It's like I'm a normal girl." I wipe the tears from my cheeks and go inside after one last kiss good night.

Jim is waiting for me inside. I'm kind of happy for the distraction. But there is something wrong. I can see it in his body language. Suddenly, I'm terrified.

"What's wrong? Is Jubal okay?" I move to his side and put a hand on his shoulder.

"Oh. I'm sorry, Ian. Jubal's fine. It's Fancy. She's lost another one of her pups. I never get used to losing a creature." Jim looks tired.

"Which puppy? Not CJ?" I regret asking immediately. It doesn't matter which pup has died. It's heartbreaking no matter.

"She's fine. It was one of the boys. He just wasn't getting enough nutrients," Jim says as he wipes his brow.

"Did you bury him?"

"No. He's in a box out back. I'll get to it here in a minute. I wanted a little break."

"I'll help you," I offer.

"No. It's okay."

"Please. I really want to."

Jim fills a thermos with coffee and grabs two flashlights from the junk drawer. He drives us in his Jeep to an area at the back of his property. We pull up to a clearing with a fire pit surrounded by a ring of chairs made out of rock and cement.

"We won't stay long enough to build a fire. Sometimes I come here to get away from everything. It's a great place to reflect." He kills the engine on the Jeep but keeps the headlights on. Together, we bury the little pup in front of a sapling, in silence.

I love this part of Jim. He's not afraid to be vulnerable. He really does love his animals. He opens the thermos and pours the coffee over the fresh mound of dirt at the base of the tree. I look at him wondering why, but don't want to embarrass him so I keep quiet.

Jim drives back to the house. "It helps the trees grow. The coffee."

"I didn't want to be rude."

"It's never rude to ask a question. I'm going to check on Fancy and her pups. Good night." Jim gives me a kiss on the head and squeezes my shoulder.

I lie in bed thinking about Sawyer. I have to meet his parents. Before insanity consumes me, I close my mind to all the thoughts fighting for my attention and fall asleep.

The day passes quickly. Sawyer parks in front of a very large and beautiful house. He takes my hand and reminds me to relax.

"Easy for you to say!"

The interior of the house looks nothing like Jim's. There is definitely a feminine touch here. I smell mulberry candles burning—my mother's favorite. My stomach clutches for a second. The walls are adorned with several photographs of the three of them. Sporting events, rodeos, Christmas photos and vacation pictures.

"Mom. We're here. It smells delish in here." Sawyer kisses his mother's cheek. "This is Ian."

"Well, hello! I'm so happy to finally meet you." Sawyer's mother wraps her plump arms around me, squeezing as she twists back and forth. "Oh, Sawyer. You are right. She is adorable."

Color floods both of our faces. She is the adorable one. She stands there in her cute, no doubt homemade, apron. I can't stop looking at her. Her makeup is soft. She wears the slightest amount of perfume. I realize I'm staring and blush again.

"It's nice to meet you, ma'am."

"Oh, please call me Patty. Ma'am is so formal."

"Where's Dad?" Sawyer asks in between snacking on a stalk of celery.

"He's probably in the family room watching

Family Feud. Go make sure he hasn't fallen asleep."
Sawyer gives me a quick smile before leaving the
kitchen.

"Can I help you with anything?" I ask.

"You can take these to the table." Patty hands me
two side dishes. As soon as I lift my hands I notice.
Patty's hands are smooth and her nails are beautifully
painted. My skin is rough and cracked. My nails are
chipped and there is a trace of oil and dirt under every
fingernail. I'm mortified. I drop my hands to my sides,
but it's too late.

"Oh, honey. Don't be embarrassed. I know a pair
of hardworking hands when I see them. After dinner I
will show you a little beauty secret." She gives me a wink
and scoots me toward the dining room.

I walk into the kitchen to find Sawyer and his
father standing by the fridge. His father has obviously
just woken up from a catnap. His hair is messy on one
side making him look like a mad scientist. I can't help but
giggle.

"Hello there. I must've nodded off."

"I'm sorry to laugh, Steve." Even though he asked
me to call him by his name, I feel awkward.

"How can you not laugh at this mess?" Sawyer
ruffles his father's hair and ducks away before he can
retaliate.

The four of us sit down to eat. Steve folds his
hands and bows his head. His wife and son follow. I've
never prayed for anything other than to escape my
father's wrath. I bow my head and put my hands in my
lap. Steve's words flow freely, like he's speaking to a
close friend, and it's so beautiful tears fill my eyes. He
asks for God to bless the food we are about to eat, but
then asks for blessings for their very special dinner guest.

He's praying for me.

Sitting here at a table with delicious food, great conversation and a beautiful family feels wonderful. I don't feel resentment or sadness. I feel truly happy. I daydream about life in Mission Valley with Jubal. I'll set the table like Patty does, with placemats and matching silverware. We'll discuss the funny answers given on *Family Feud.* I'll tell him a silly joke the delivery guy made when dropping off the new air compressor to the garage.

"I wish you could've been here for Sawyer's party. Patty did a great job putting it together." Steve pats his wife's hand.

"I wasn't ready to be embarrassed in front of you so I wouldn't let her send you an invite. I hope you understand," Sawyer tries to whisper.

This makes me giggle. "It's all right, Sawyer. I understand."

I offer to help with the dishes but Steve tells me he and Sawyer will take care of the cleanup. Patty's eyes light up, as she whisks me upstairs to her bedroom. There must be a hundred pillows on their bed. The curtains match the floral design of the comforter. Her bathroom is enormous. They each have their own sink. She begins to pull fancy-looking bottles from a cabinet, pouring a little of each into a bowl.

"Sit here at the vanity. I do this when the seasons change or after a long day of gardening. Here, soak your hands in this." She guides my hands into the warm soapy mixture.

Patty has about fifty different colors of fingernail polish. She picks up one from each color. "This is Berry Bubble. This one is very pretty. It's called Truly Tickled Pink. Oh, how about Redhead Envy?"

"What one do you think will look best? I've never done this."

"You've never had a manicure?"

"I've never even painted my nails."

"Well then... this is going to be a treat for both of us because I've never given a manicure!" Patty laughs in excitement.

We meet the guys in the family room after Patty fixes two nails I manage to smudge without doing a single thing but breathing. I felt horrible about it, until she explained that it happens all the time.

I sit next to Sawyer, holding my hands out like a puppy begging for scraps. He looks at me with a huge grin.

"Say one word and I'll wipe this still wet polish all over you!"

"I won't say a word. That's a nice color."

"It's Truly Tickled Pink. And I had to talk her into it. She preferred clear." Patty winks at me before settling into her recliner.

I thank them for a great evening.

"We can't wait to have you back here. You take care of yourself." Patty gives me an extra-long squeeze.

Sawyer pulls out of the driveway waving to his parents. "I think my mom is worried that you'll never come back."

"I kinda have that feeling also. She gave me an extra-long hug goodbye. She's great."

"She is. She really had fun spending time with you. I knew they'd love you."

Sawyer holds my hand, rubbing his thumb along my hand the whole way back to Jim's. We find Jim out back, a nice fire going in a steel pit, telling stories with Marcus and Ricky.

"Hey, guys! How was the trip? I wasn't sure you'd make it back before I'd have to leave."

We visit for just a few minutes. Sawyer and I both have to get up early. We tell the men good night before going inside.

"It's kind of weird being in your room." Sawyer stays in the doorway, peeking over his shoulder waiting for Jim to show up.

"You can relax. Jim trusts us."

"I'm not sure I do." Sawyer steps close to me, pulling me into his arms with a cute evil laugh.

"I am going to miss you so much. I've had a great visit. And before you know it, I'll be here for good. How cool is that?"

"It's the coolest!" Sawyer's lips meet mine and time stands still.

Our bodies move as one onto the bed. My leg tangles with his. Sawyer pulls away and smiles widely. I smile back. "I guess it's a good thing the door is open."

We don't move. We just lie there talking and kissing… well, more kissing than talking. Sawyer's eyes grow heavy. "I better get going."

"No. Please stay. I won't let you fall asleep. Please?"

"Okay. I'll stay with you, Ian."

~~~~~~~

I wake to daylight breaking through the window. I don't have to turn my head to know that Sawyer is still next to me. I notice two things. We are covered under a blanket and the door is closed. Panic sets in.

"Sawyer. Sawyer!" I nudge his arm but he only rolls over and pulls me in for a hug. "Sawyer!"

"Good morning, beautiful." He stretches and rubs his eyes before sitting straight up.

"Why didn't you wake me up?" I try to tame my crazy hair but by the way Sawyer's eyes are locked in on my messy coif, I must be failing.

"Wake *you* up? Why didn't *you* wake *me* up?"

"Oh, shit." I am up pacing the floor. "Jim was here. He covered us up."

"Okay. You go downstairs and I'll climb out the window. It's been nice knowing you."

We both crack up laughing, trying to be as quiet as possible. It's not quiet enough.

"Breakfast is on the table," Jim calls out, and knocks on the door. I think I hear him laughing, too.

Sawyer grabs me and gives me a sweet kiss. "I loved waking up next to you."

We walk into the kitchen with our heads down. I want to apologize but I'm so embarrassed I can't make eye contact. Nothing happened, but I still feel horrible.

"Oh, stop it. You fell asleep on top of the covers. No big deal. I let your mom know you were staying over, Sawyer. Now, sit down and eat… *lovebirds*."

Chapter Fourteen

I pull into the garage at the ranch and all but sprint into the house. Jubal is on the couch watching another Western. I hop onto the cushion next to him and wrap my arms around his neck.

"I had the best time! I wish you'd gone. Jim really misses you. He sends his love. So does Sawyer. They want us to come for the annual town picnic. Sawyer's parents are super- nice. So, how were things without me?" Overflowing with excitement, I forget to breathe.

Jubal looks at me without expression. "Well, I went to work at Sylvia's and broke up three fights. I watched endless amounts of television. And then I cleaned like mad because I was so bored in this quiet house." He tries to mock my excitement but it doesn't work.

"I guess I win. Where's Mikus?"

"He had to do some things for Julio. Haven't seen him since he showed up at camp."

I tell him more about my visit. Jubal raises his eyebrows when I tell him about Sawyer falling asleep in my room. I have to repeat myself twice that nothing happened.

I offer to cook, but Jubal tells me he's made a batch of his chili. He's also made a cake and two different types of cookies. "I told you I was bored."

We spend the rest of the day watching his beloved Westerns and napping. I'm not glad to be back at the ranch but I missed Jubal so much. And he missed me. The thought of him in an apron like Patty's makes me laugh.

After eating more cookies than we should, we say good night and I head to my room. I'm halfway down the hall when I hear his tired voice coming from the living room. "I'm glad you're home."

As much I love staying at Jim's house, it just feels right crawling into my own bed. I lie here thinking about Sawyer. Suddenly, my heart is heavy. I'm reminded I didn't tell Sawyer the truth about what I'm doing for Mikus—or the truth about my parents. The guilty feeling only lasts for a moment. His smiling face pushes the thoughts from my mind.

I wake early to make Jubal a special breakfast. He loves my banana pancakes. I reach for the griddle and the ingredients. When I close the cupboard Mikus is leaning on the counter.

"Holy shit, Mikus! You scared me to death."

"If only. I thought I'd have some peace and quiet when I got home, but here you are."

"The feeling is mutual."

I go about my business and start Jubal's pancakes. Mikus grabs his breakfast from the fridge. It's his last beer so he grabs another case from the pantry to chill before leaving to the garage. I know he can't see me but I stick my tongue out at him anyway.

Jubal devours the pancakes. He seems disappointed when I tell him about Mikus being home.

"How's his mood?"

"Same as always towards me. He's out in the garage."

"Remember, Ian. We are on our way out. Please try to keep the peace. I'm counting on you."

That's a lot of pressure. It's not always my fault. I just smile and promise to try. The door opens and I look at Jubal with rolling eyes. He raises his eyebrows to remind me of my promise.

"Hey, Mikus. How's business?"

"This is going to be a money-maker. I'm so

stoked! We'll bank fifty grand easy." It's obvious he spent less time weighing the drugs and more time doing them.

Jubal puts his dishes in the sink and leaves the room. I bite my tongue and follow him into the living room. Mikus flies in after me.

"Don't be like this, man. I've got it under control. Besides, you're out soon anyway. I've got it under control." His wild hair and dilated pupils say otherwise.

We spend a few hours finishing weighing out the coke and going over the drops. The majority is for regulars but there are a handful of new deliveries that Jubal questions. Mikus brushes them off saying they are college kids and some new business associates.

Our drive to Reno is surprisingly fun. The three of us share silly stories and corny jokes. Mikus is in the best mood I've seen in a long time. His moods change so quickly.

"I think we should go see a movie. I'll buy."

Jubal looks at me and smiles, as if Mikus is showing me his real personality. The Mikus O'Malley that Jubal has loved like a brother and protected for years.

"That sounds great, Mikus!" I say, and I mean it. I've been wanting to see the new James Bond movie.

I hop out of the Blazer, straighten my pastel slacks and ugly sweater, and then make my way into the Circus Circus. I walk in step with all of the families, as I've done so many times before. But I no longer wish I had what they have. I see the kids rolling their eyes at their fathers. I see teens scheming to get away from their drunken mothers. I used to see perfect families. Now, I know there is no such thing as a perfect family. You have to make the most out of what you have. Or, as in my case, find the family you were meant to have.

The elevator door opens at the seventeenth floor. Two security guards board the elevator. I'm riding to the nineteenth floor. I think about getting off and taking another elevator, but it's too late. The doors are closing.

"Eighteen," the guard says.

"Eighteen," the second guard says a moment later.

"Oh. Sorry." I reach forward and push the button for the eighteenth floor and stare at my feet.

The two guards go on about their conversation over some game. I try to steady my breathing. My shoes are ugly. Who thought up jelly shoes, anyway?

The elevator dings and the doors open. The guards step out, still engrossed in chatter about the overtime winning basket. I take a deep breath and laugh to myself. "It's not like they're cops."

Knock twice. Pause. Knock twice. Pause. Knock three times. I've got this routine down. This is where I shine. I'm at ease and willing to sell as much as they have money to buy. A woman opens the door. She looks nothing like any of my other customers—she looks like Patty. A housewife. Beautifully manicured nails, perfectly styled hair, mom-clothes. There goes my game.

"Come on in. I'm not sure how this works. I have the money in my purse." The lady tucks her hair behind her ear and turns away from me.

I'm so confused. Mikus said he had a few new customers, but I didn't realize he'd meant new to drugs. I don't know what to say so I remain silent.

"I have two hundred. I'm not sure how much it'll get, though, so I'll just have to trust you."

"Here." I hand her a package.

"Thank you. You aren't what I expected."

"You either. Is this your first time doing coke?" My curiosity gets the best of me.

"It's not for me." She places the package into her purse.

"Oh shit! Are you a cop?" I step towards the door.

"No. I'm not a cop. I'm a mother. This is for my son." Tears well up in this stranger's eyes.

"I don't understand."

"He's so sick. He was trying to get clean. My husband told him this was his last chance. His body is so weak. He's so sick." Her hands are trembling and the tears that have flooded her eyes, now trail down her cheeks.

"I still don't understand. Why are you here?"

"He's sick. If I don't get this for him, he's going to die. He just needs a little bit to stop the withdrawal symptoms."

I understand now. My stomach is in knots. I don't know what to do or say. I have the money. She has the drugs.

"I should go."

"How do you live with yourself?" She isn't angry. She's defeated.

"You'd be surprised at what I have to live with," I reply. Then, as an afterthought: "I hope your son gets better."

The elevator is not moving fast enough. I push open the door to the stairway and sprint down the eighteen flights. I want to keep running out of the casino but I can't draw attention to myself. I straighten up before pushing open the door and getting lost in the masses of people on the casino floor.

I rush to Sylvia's to find Jubal. When I walk in, it's Mikus who notices me first. He pounces on me in seconds. "What the hell are you doing here? There were more drops to make."

"Shut up, Mikus!" I push past him and continue into the bar until I'm standing in front of Jubal.

"What happened? *Are you okay*?" Jubal is screaming his questions so I can hear over the music.

"Come here." I lead him to the back door. We step out into the alley. I'm about to explain what happened when Mikus joins us.

"What the hell is going on?" Mikus is pacing with his wild red hair and bulging veins.

"I needed to take a break. The delivery was to a mother. Like, a Betty Crocker-looking mother. She was buying drugs for her son. She asked me how I could live with myself. I freaked out. I've always been able to deliver without questioning myself. It's always been druggies on the other side of the door." I'm focusing on Jubal's face, trying to explain how this impacted me.

"So, you have a conscience? *Who gives a shit*?" Mikus takes a chug of his Bud and tosses the can into the dumpster.

"Mikus. Go inside and get another drink. I'll get her straightened out and we'll finish the deliveries."

Mikus leaves after a few choice words for me.

"It was awful. I can't even get her face out of my head. She would do anything for her son. She thought buying him drugs was going to save his life. She was so sad, Jubal." I can't help the tears that spill onto my cheeks.

"I get it. I'll finish the drops." Jubal rubs his forehead in frustration.

"I'm fine! I just needed to vent. This is bullshit! I'm out of here." I run down the alley with adrenaline coursing through my veins.

The rest of my drops are made on autopilot. I do not make eye contact or work my usual charm. I do what

I have to do to get the job done. I'm in the Blazer pretending to be asleep in the back seat when the guys get in. Jubal reaches back and tugs the blanket over me before firing up the engine.

"I'm telling you, dude. She's gotta go. We've got a good thing going. I'm back in good with Julio. The money will start rolling in now. I don't see why you think your life is going to be a bed of roses following that little girl." Mikus turns his head, making sure I'm not awake.

"Mikus, I hear what you're saying. I've wanted to do this long before Ian showed up. Why do you hate her so much? She never did anything to you."

"Except stab me with a fork."

I roll over to face the back of the seat, hiding the smile on my face. He's such a puke. I listen to him yammer on about his bullshit fantasy until we pull into the garage. I wait for Jubal to nudge my leg before sitting up and stretching.

"Here, Mikus." I hand him the money from tonight's drops. "I'm sorry I freaked out." I try to convince him I was sleeping by not punching him in the mouth.

I walk straight to my room, locking the door behind me. The world can kiss my ass. I watch the clock on my nightstand change from one hour to the next, unable to turn off my brain. When I close my eyes I'm haunted by thoughts of the mother in the hotel room. When I open them, I hear the words Mikus spewed about what a piece of shit I am. Jubal put him in his place, but it stings a little that he didn't drop him off on the side of the highway.

Hunger forces me out of my room around two o'clock. I quietly walk to the kitchen and make a bowl of cereal. I look out the window to see Mikus in the garage.

"Asshole."

"Good afternoon to you, too." Jubal laughs.

"Hey, Jubal."

"Do you have any questions?" Jubal doesn't look at me as he tops off his coffee mug. He knows I wasn't sleeping in the Blazer last night.

"No. I expected every word out of his stupid mouth. I'm so tired. I didn't sleep last night. I can't stop thinking about that woman."

Jubal walks over to me and places one of his large calloused hands on my shoulder. "It won't be long, now. There's a light at the end of the tunnel."

I need at least two pots of coffee to keep me awake today. Tonight is going to be brutal. I just hope there are no more mothers.

Chapter Fifteen

"Stop pouting. It's a short night. Only a handful of drops." Mikus hops into the passenger seat and flicks his cigarette out the window.

"I'm not pouting. I'm just tired." I lie down to try and get some sleep before we get to Reno.

I'm so glad this is almost over. I never really thought of the morality of what I was doing. I just wondered if I'd get caught. If it's possible, I hate myself a little more now after seeing the despair on the woman's face.

Jubal parks behind Sylvia's. I finish what's left of my coffee and climb out. I pull the backpack on and look at Mikus.

"Just these four?" I look at the coded list. Mikus weighed this order after I went to my room last night. I usually write out the list myself. His chicken scratch is hard to read.

"Yes, three new ones tonight. Trevor has a big order. You'll stop by JoJo's last." Mikus disappears inside.

"Ian. Are you sure you're up to this?"

"I'm fine. I just need to make the first drop and let the adrenaline take over. I'll see you by eight-thirty, nine at the latest." I leave before he can see the tears welling up in my eyes.

I walk slower than usual, noticing every crack in the sidewalk, every cigarette butt, every wad of gum. I don't want to think about anything or anyone. I just focus on the filthy city sidewalks.

The elevator climbs to the twelfth floor. Nobody joins me. I'm thankful for the silence. I look at the list again. I stand in front of 1283. Knock twice. Pause. Knock twice. Pause. Knock three times. "Please don't be her. Please don't be her."

The door swings open and I'm flooded with relief.
A balding shirtless man and his prostitute invite me in.
The hooker likes to call me "Sugar". I put on my cutest
smile and make the deal. The guy can't get rid of me fast
enough. The hooker is sad to see me go. I feel sorry for
her.

The next stop is in a suite. A very handsome man
opens the door in a towel, fresh from the shower. His skin
is tan and soft. It looks like he's removed all of his body
hair. He mistakes my blushing for attraction, when
actually I'm uncomfortable being alone with him.
Thankfully, there are two naked ladies on the bed. Why
do drugs and weirdoes seemingly go hand-in-hand? This
is the big player. He hands me a thick wad of cash and I
turn over the large bundle. "You like to party?" he says.
The towel now lies on the floor at his feet.

"Thanks, but I already have penis ... I mean
plans." I can't help but glance at his package and wonder
if Sawyer's looks similar. My face reddens.

"All right, ladies. Let's get this party started." The
guy gives me a wink and turns his back to me. His butt is
even hairless.

"What the hell is wrong with people?" I walk out,
laughing to myself all the way outside.

The last two drops are just a few blocks from
Sylvia's. I pick up my pace. I can't wait to get this night
over with. I need a few days to get my head straight.
Maybe Jubal will take me camping again.

I get to the Second Street Inn and climb the stairs
to the second floor. This is a far cry from the suite I just
left. I stop in front of 203. Knock twice. Pause. Knock…
The door opens to a guy not much older than Sawyer. His
collar is stiff and his jeans are tight. His Vans are brand

new. He looks out of place here.

"Come in. I'm a little anxious. I've been waiting over an hour. This is Jimmy." He points to a guy that could be his twin.

"You know there's a reason we have a certain knock." I put my hand in my pocket to keep it from shaking.

"Sorry. You'll have to excuse Wilson. He's not the most patient person." Jimmy walks over and holds out his hand to shake mine. I adjust my backpack instead.

"Wilson, you've upset our guest."

"No. I'm fine. Do you have the money?" I want out of here now.

"What did you say your name is?" Wilson is now at the table counting out twenties.

"I didn't. Can we just make the deal, already?"

The tower, consisting of empty beer cans and a half-empty vodka bottle, sets me on edge. Jimmy picks up on my body language. "Dude, give her the money. I need a line."

Wilson hands me a pile of twenties. I count them out then hand him the blow. He walks over to the table so I reach for the doorknob. A hand stops the door from opening. I expect to see Wilson but it's Jimmy who's standing two inches from my face, breath reeking of alcohol. I thrust a fist into his throat. He drops to his knees.

I pull again at the doorknob but he grabs me by the hair and throws me on the floral comforter.

"You shouldn't be so rude to your hosts. See, we are ready to party." Jimmy looks over to Wilson. "Line us up."

"I'm sorry I hit you. I panicked. Please let me go. They are expecting me back now. You're my last stop." I feel vomit making its way up into my throat.

"I'll make this quick. You see, I wasn't expecting such a pretty little thing when I placed this order." He moves the strands of hair covering my face, tucking it behind my ear.

Wilson snorts his line, rubbing the residual onto his gums. "Your turn. It's good shit."

"I don't do drugs anymore," I lie, all the while struggling to get out of Jimmy's grip.

I'm jerked to my feet and led to the table. Wilson hands me a straw. I look down to the small square mirror with several lines laid out. Wilson is sitting behind the table and Jimmy is at my back. He is the only thing standing between me and the door. I take the straw then lean down to snort a line.

"Oh, I knew she was down." Jimmy high-fives Wilson.

I grab the mirror, dumping the coke and spin around catching Jimmy on the cheek. I make it to the door, open it and make one foot out of the door before the world goes black.

I open my eyes and see Wilson handing Jimmy a washcloth. I try to move but I'm unable to. My brain is telling my body to get up but it won't.

"Dude, let's get out of here. She looks dead. You beat the shit out of her." Wilson is lining up more one more line for each of them.

"No. I'm not quite finished. She's feisty. I like that." He jumps on top of me, straddling my hips.

I lift my hands to fight him off but he easily grabs them with one hand, punching me in the mouth with his free hand. I hear my lip pop as my teeth puncture it.

"So, you're a cutter?" He traces the cut on his cheek with bony fingers. "I've never been a cutter. I'm more of a biter." He leans down and bites me hard on my chest.

I scream, but he covers my face with his hand. "I just wanted to have a little fun. But no, you had to be a bitch. All you girls are bitches."

"That's only because you have a little dick." Wilson laughs.

"Screw you, dude. Your mom never complains." Jimmy throws an empty beer can in his direction.

I'm swallowing a lot of blood. I turn my head to vomit. This enrages him, and before I know it he's yanking me from the bed and he throws me into the door. "You threw up on me!" He pulls me by the hair into the bathroom. I hit my side hard on the bathtub, falling to the floor. I'm laying half in the bathroom and half out. I look up at Wilson for help but he notices nothing but the cocaine.

"Please! Please, let me go. I'm sorry. I'm sorry I was a bitch." Tears spill onto my face.

Jimmy looks at me with a crooked sneer then steps on my left arm. I can hear it break. The world around me fades in and out. I can hear them talking but can't make out all of the words.

"Make me another line, dude."

"No. We've gotta get out of here."

"I said I'm not done with her yet." He unbuckles his belt and takes a step towards me.

"This wasn't part of the deal. The plan was to scare her and mess her up a little—nothing about rape. Now I said, let's go!"

Jimmy kneels down, licking my face. "I guess this is your lucky day." He leaves me but not before grabbing me by the throat and pushing me into the floor. I lose consciousness again.

I pull myself up with my right hand. The guys have left—at least, I don't see them and the door is wide open. I have no idea what time it is. They took my backpack. Mikus is going to be pissed. My left hand is at a weird angle. I'm covered in blood. I slowly step towards the door, catching a glimpse of myself in the mirror above the table. I don't even recognize myself. I vomit on the floor, not wanting to go back into the bathroom and away from the door.

I have to get to Jubal. Leaning on the brick exterior of this shitty motel, I make my way down the stairs. I'm glad this didn't happen inside one of the casinos, Security would notice me immediately. I can't remember the way to Sylvia's. But, it doesn't matter, because I don't remember the number or have any change for the payphone. I straighten my hair and wipe some of the blood from my face. My steps are uneven. I must look drunk, staggering along the dark streets. The sidewalk is swaying back and forth. I fall onto a bench.

"I'll just rest for a little bit and then go find Jubal." After giving myself permission, I close my eyes to stop the world from spinning.

I hear a car approaching. The bright lights and screech of the brakes wake me. I'm on my feet trying to escape. "Get away from me! Get away!"

"Holy shit! Ian! It's me. It's Jubal."

I'm lifted into his arms. "Mikus, drive." He climbs into the passenger seat with me in his lap. "Get us to the emergency room."

"No. I can't. They'll call my parents. Please. Take me home," I say.

"Ian. I can't fix this!" Jubal's voice catches in his throat.

"We can take her to Doctor Feldman."

Jubal asks questions, lots of questions. I try to answer but I just want to sleep.

"Thank you, guys. Thank you for finding me. Thank you for saving me," I mumble as Jubal rocks me back and forth softly. I can feel his heart beating. "Mikus, they took it. They took it all."

"It's okay. Don't worry about that. You just try to stay awake. We'll be there soon."

"Who was it?" Jubal's emotions are changing from shock to sadness to anger. "Who was it, Mikus?"

"It was just some college kids. Rich college kids… I thought they'd be good for business."

"I'm sorry. I tried to fight back, Jubal. I tried…"

My words trail off as I give into the beauty that is sleep.

~~~~~~~~

I can feel Jubal getting out of the Blazer. The air is chilly. I try to open my eyes but I can't. I don't know if I'm too tired or if they are swollen shut. I guess it's both.

Mikus is banging on the door. "Doc. Open up. It's Mikus."

A few moments later Jubal is carrying me inside. I can hear them talking but I can't make out the words. I vomit down Jubal's front and hear it splatter on the floor.

"What the hell, Mikus?" Dr. Feldman stands there in his silk pajamas. "What are you doing here? My wife is upstairs."

"Well, then. I guess we shouldn't wake her. It'd be a little awkward having your drug dealer in the living room."

Dr. Feldman takes a quick look at me and frowns. "I have to turn this in. She's been assaulted. You found her like this?"

"Please. Fix her." Jubal is pleading.

"Jubal, I can't set a fracture here. We have to go to my clinic."

We are back on the road but only for a short time. I think it's a short time. It could be a lifetime. Jubal carries me through the doorway of what smells like a hospital. I stir in his arms.

"Shhh. It's okay. It's Dr. Feldman's clinic. We're safe here. He thinks you have a broken arm."

"He stepped on me."

Jubal says nothing. He just weeps.

"Miss? Do you think you are able to change into a robe?" Dr. Feldman asks me in a soft voice.

I grab onto Jubal's arm. I don't want to take my clothes off. Panic is consuming me. I'm struggling to get away.

"Ian. It's okay. It's okay." Jubal is singing his words. Soothing me. "You're safe now. Do you want me to leave so the doctor can help you?"

"Don't leave me. Please, Jubal. Don't leave me." Together, the two of us manage to get me out of my ripped and bloodied clothes while Dr. Feldman steps out to question Mikus.

"What the hell is that?" Jubal no longer speaks in a singsong whisper. "Is that a bite mark?"

I nod.

My body aches and stings and throbs. I'm dizzy. My heart is breaking for Jubal. I know this is killing him. I can hear it when he speaks. I can hear it when he breathes the snot back into his nostrils. I can tell when his tears fall onto my skin.

"Did they…?" Jubal can't form the words to complete his question.

"No. One of them wanted to but the other guy

stopped him."

Dr. Feldman returns. He examines me head to toe, writing his findings in a chart. The X-ray confirms a break.

"I'm going to give you something to help with the pain. I need to set your arm and put you in a cast." Dr. Feldman pats my shoulder softly. Two seconds later, the world again goes black.

Chapter Sixteen

"Jubal?" I try to sit up but a hand grasps my arm. Jubal's hand.

"Shh. I'm here. We're home, in your room. Let me turn this light on." He releases my arm and leans to turn on a small nightlight.

I blink my eyes rapidly until the dim light no longer hurts. "I feel like I got hit by a truck."

"You look even worse." Jubal gives me a small grin.

"As long as I don't look as bad as you. When's the last time you've showered? Or shaved?" I touch his scruffy face with the back of my hand. "Shit. Even my hand is bruised."

"Do you remember what happened?"

"Some of it. Most of it is cloudy. I'm okay." The slightest movement causes me to grimace in pain.

"It's been five days. Five days. I picked up the phone to call Jim like a hundred times."

"You didn't call him … please tell me you didn't call him. I'm okay, Jubal. I'm okay."

"I didn't know that. I thought you were gonna die. I never made the call. I didn't know what to say. Dr. Feldman kept you in his office for three days. You were on fluids and some antibiotics."

"Antibiotics for what?"

Jubal shifts uncomfortably in the recliner he moved in from his room. "The bite."

"Tell me everything."

"I don't think you want to hear it."

"I can take it. This isn't the first beating I've had, Jubal."

"That makes it even worse." Jubal wipes a tear from his cheek.

"Seriously? Don't be a baby." I try to laugh but it's excruciating.

Jubal reads through the list of diagnoses. When he reaches the end I smile.

"What in the hell are you smiling for?"

"Jubal. I don't think I've ever been out for five days, but that could be from the pain medicine the doctor has me on. I've had surgery on my spleen, bruised kidneys, two broken fingers and a broken leg. Not to mention the countless bruises, cuts and scrapes. But I'm okay. I'm sorry I scared you." I'm not ready for Jubal's reaction. He squeezes my hand, buries his head in my covers and lets out a cry that I'm sure he's held in since he found me on the street. "I'm sorry, Jubal."

"You the best person I know. I'm serious, man. You lying here on the brink of death and *you* the one sorry! Can I get you some food or something to drink? I had Mikus load the house with all of your favorites. There's 7up, chocolate pudding, cottage cheese, chocolate milk. You name it." Before I know it Jubal is up and waiting for my reply.

"I'm not hungry. Chocolate milk sounds good." I can tell Jubal just needs a break from his emotions.

"I'm so glad you woke up. I was so scared."

I can only whisper the words. "Thank you, Jubal. Thank you for saving my life. Again."

Jubal leaves and I immediately begin to doze off. I refuse to succumb to sleep for fear of losing another five days, and instead slowly slide my legs over the side of the bed. The room spins slowly. Vomit threatens my throat. I take a deep breath and calm my pulse before standing. My legs are weak but hold me upright. I shuffle to the window. Jubal's Blazer is parked right by the kitchen door. I imagine it's been parked there since he carried me inside two nights ago.

I do feel horrible to have worried him these past five nights. I have felt worse, though. This doesn't compare to what I had at home at the hands of my father. Strangers and monsters are the ones who should pose a threat, not a parent.

When Jubal returns he's surprised to see me standing by the window. "Get back into bed. What are you thinking? You need to rest. Dr. Feldman says so." He holds a tray full of drinks and snacks to choose from.

"I have to use the bathroom before I climb back in. Can you help me?" My face blushes with embarrassment.

"Who do you think has been taking care of you this whole time?" Jubal smiles at me. "Just so you know, you wipe from the front to the rear to prevent infection. Dr. Feldman taught me that."

"That's not the most embarrassing thing I've ever heard, but it's close." I let Jubal take my arm and lead me to the bathroom across the hall.

Jubal tucks me in bed and points to a deep bruise on my forearm. "See that scratch and bruise? Those are because of me."

"Jubal, this wasn't your fault." I take his hand in mine.

"No, I mean it. I dropped you on the way upstairs." He winks at me.

I laugh, but it's too much. I wince in pain. "Jubal! You're so bad. Did you really drop me?"

"No. I wanted you to smile." He grabs the tray and holds it in front of me. "Take a drink and a snack."

"Where's Mikus? Is he pissed?" I reach for a chocolate milk and pudding.

"He's been in Reno working for Julio. He feels

real bad about this. When you didn't show up at Sylvia's he couldn't remember the motel you were dropping to. He just remembered the street. I was driving around for two hours looking for you."

There's a noise coming from the hallway. I assume it's Mikus and my heart starts to sink, when suddenly I hear a voice. "Jubal? Ian? Where are you?" Jim calls out to us.

"*You called him*?" I pull the covers high up to my neck. I'm not embarrassed that he sees me in a tank top and underwear. I'm afraid of his reaction when he sees the condition I'm in.

"I didn't call him. I didn't." Jubal meets his brother at the door.

Jim takes one look at my bruised face, and his own turns beet red. "What in the hell? What happened? Did Mikus do this to you?"

"No. Jim, I'm okay." The mixture of purple and blue covering the left side of my face begs to differ.

"Tell me now. You tell me what happened to this little girl, Jubal." Jim is standing with clenched fists, demanding an explanation.

"Jim." Jubal is frozen to the spot, unable to think of an excuse.

Moments pass, and I swear Jim might explode if he doesn't get an answer soon.

"She laid a bike down. Chicks shouldn't ride. I told 'em both a thousand times. Bitches can't drive. They belong on the back. That's why it's called riding Bitch." Mikus appears out of nowhere with the story. He doesn't join us in my room. He continues walking down the hall without another word.

"What are you doing here, Jim?" Jubal's

shoulders relax a little now that we have an excuse, at least for the time being.

"You missed the Annual Picnic. I tried to call a few times and was worried when there was no word so I decided to make the trip down and see why ya'll weren't there." Jim sits on the edge of the bed carefully.

I'm wondering why this couldn't have happened after the picnic. Now, there are two people who are worrying about me.

"We were going to call you today. It's the first day she's felt decent enough to hold a telephone." Jubal looks at his brother with pleading eyes.

Jim can tell by my injuries and Jubal's lack of personal hygiene that what he says is true.

"How's Fancy and CJ? How are the guys? What about the ranch? Are things okay? Have you talked to Sawyer?" I realize I'm spitting out too many questions and lie back on my pillow.

"Whoa. The pups and mama are all great. The pups all have their forever homes set up. The guys are working as hard as ever. The ranch is the same as you left it." He turns to the doorway. "Sawyer," Jim calls out into the hallway.

"Sawyer's *here*?" I look to Jubal and back to Jim. "You brought Sawyer? He can't see me like this." I try to pull the covers up over my head but the motion causes me too much pain.

Jim walks to the door and talks to Sawyer before he walks in. I'm thinking Jim is trying to prepare him for what he's about to see. It won't work. I saw my reflection when Jubal took me to the bathroom. I'm hideous.

"Ian." That is the only word Sawyer can manage to get out.

Jim nods to Jubal and the two men leave us alone.

"What in the world?"

"It looks worse than it feels. Honest. I'll be back to normal in no time." I give Sawyer a reassuring smile. "I lost your ring. It must've fallen off in the accident."

Sawyer climbs onto the bed and holds me softly. He doesn't speak. He just holds me. I feel his body tremble and I know he's crying. I let him cry. I weave my fingers through his hair. I've missed his smell. I've missed his touch. I fall asleep in his arms.

I dream about the motel. The two guys are there but they have faces like rats. Dirty rodents that scavenge through garbage finding anything they can smoke, snort or inject. I'm chained to a filthy mattress. My head is pounding. I try to get free but one of the rats crawls on top of me and bites me. I'm struggling to get away but I can't. It hurts too much.

"Ian. Wake up, Ian. You're okay. Wake up." Sawyer is still lying next to me, looking scared as ever.

Jubal stomps upstairs and into my room. "What's wrong?"

"I'm okay. I fell asleep and had a bad dream."

"Rats again? Okay, guys. It's time to go. She needs her rest. I promise we'll get in touch with you as soon as she's had time to fully recuperate," Jubal says in a way they know not to question.

"Sawyer, let's go. I'll be downstairs while you say goodbye." Jim leans down and touches my cast. He closes his eyes like he's holding in a rant. When he opens his eyes he looks at me with sadness before kissing my forehead. "I'll see you soon, sweetheart."

"Okay. I can't wait. Give Fancy a squeeze for me and tell CJ to be good for her new family." I hold Jim's hand, not wanting to let go.

Jubal and Jim leave us once again. Sawyer hasn't

moved from my bed. He kisses my bruised face, starting at my forehead followed by my swollen cheek and ending at my lips. I kiss him back. My head feels as if it is going to split open, but I kiss him until he pulls away.

"I don't want to leave you. I'll call you when I get home. I'm going to call you every night. I'm sorry this happened to you. Promise me you'll stick to driving your car and no more motorcycles?" Sawyer kisses me once again before climbing out of bed.

I feel guilty for not telling them the truth. I can't risk losing them. Jim would be so disappointed. Sawyer might realize he is so much better off without me. I can't take that chance. He loves me. I don't know what I'd do if he were to stop loving me.

I wait for a minute before crawling out of bed and looking out my window. Tears fill my eyes as I watch two of the most important people in my life get into a pickup and drive away. Jubal waves goodbye and hangs his head, standing still on the porch for several minutes before stepping inside.

"They gone?" Mikus stands in my doorway.

I realize I'm in my underwear so I slide into bed as gingerly as possible. "Yep. Thanks for having our backs." I don't want to look at him anymore. "Please shut my door. I'm really tired."

I sip the chocolate milk. It has no flavor. I set the glass on the nightstand and close my eyes. I don't want to fall asleep and see the rats again. A while later Jubal knocks softly on the door before joining me.

"Would you like a shower? I have a seat to put in the tub for you."

"I can see a shower did wonders for you. I don't even recognize you! The hairy beast is gone!" I give a small giggle.

"Yuk it up. I'd have been able to shower if I wasn't glued to your bedside for the last five days." He sees my lips curl into a frown and regrets his joke immediately.

"Jubal. Seriously, stop being a baby. I'm okay. I'm not going to break. I'm afraid to sleep, though." I look at Jubal's recliner. "How'd you know about the rats?"

"You've been reliving that night every time you close your eyes. I had Mikus move the chair in here before I brought you home. I knew where I'd be living until you got well." Jubal points to his oversized leather recliner.

I take Jubal up on the offer to help me into the shower. He puts a garbage bag over my arm to keep it dry. The shower chair is perfect. I sit there until the water runs cool. Jubal helps me dress and get back into bed before going to take care of a few things.

"I'll be back in a little bit. Want me to bring you anything?"

"No thanks. I'm okay. The pain pills are kicking in so I'll be out cold in no time." Jubal can see the look of worry on my face. "I'll be okay. I promise."

~~~~~~~~

I must've slept for hours because when I open my eyes I can see the orange glow of sunset in the window. I'm thankful I didn't wake up sweaty and afraid. The rats didn't take my sleep this time. Maybe they're gone for good.

I slowly shuffle my way to the bathroom and stand in front of the mirror, looking at my features. I despise drugs. Drugs make people do horrible things. I deserved this for delivering the drugs to them. This is my punishment. "I'll never do it again. I'm sorry."

Mikus is standing in the hallway outside the bathroom. "Can I bring you anything?"

I cross the hallway into my room. "No, thanks." I notice Mikus' face is full of freckles. He looks years younger without the scowl that is usually a permanent fixture.

Mikus speaks in a voice I've not heard him use. It's friendly. I need all the friends I can get right now. "Thank you, Mikus." I crawl into bed, angry the slightest physical activity causes such fatigue.

"I feel bad this happened to you, Ian. I had no idea. I've been lookin' for those punks." Mikus sinks into Jubal's recliner.

"Don't waste your time. You'll just get into trouble. I'm okay. You guys were there for me. I'm glad you know Dr. Feldman." I hold up my cast and give him a grin.

"Did they say anything? The guys."

"I don't remember. I keep trying to piece it together, but it hurts my head."

"It's probably best that you focus on *you*, and get well." Mikus gets out of the chair with a bit of a struggle.

"I'm sorry they took my backpack. All the money was in there."

"Don't worry about that. I'll figure it out." The scowl returns to his face. "I'll figure it out."

Chapter Seventeen

"It's been three weeks, Jubal. I'm going crazy. I need to get out of here." I stand in the kitchen with my keys in hand.

"I ain't your warden or your daddy. Dr. Feldman said you have to rest for six to eight weeks. If you think you know better than the doctor, go." Jubal continues stirring the chili on the stove.

I throw the keys on the table and return to my room. The walls get smaller and smaller every day. Even with the little television that Jubal moved into my room, I'm bored out of my mind. I know it's not Jubal's fault. I feel horrible for taking it out on him. I return to the kitchen.

"Have you lost your mind? There is no way. Shut up about it." Jubal stands at the stove, one hand stirring and the other is pointed in Mikus' face.

"What's going on in here?" I grab a roll from the basket on the table, adding a thick layer of butter.

"Hey, Ian. Nothing. I was talking to Jubal about getting back to business. He's not interested." Mikus grabs a beer from the fridge.

I notice his tic is back. It's a small twitch he gets when he's been using. His head jerks slightly to his right shoulder. I can only guess what business he was talking about. The kindhearted caring Mikus didn't stick around long.

"Are you kidding me? I just stopped pissing blood last week and you want me back on the streets? No way." My brain pounds against the inside of my skull.

"Ian. Go lie down. I told you to rest. Don't worry about this. It's not going to happen." Jubal points the spoon in the direction of my bedroom.

"Fine. Bring me a bowl of chili and the dice. I'm

bored out of my mind." I turn to make a fabulous exit but end up bumping into the wall. Stupid concussion.

Jubal enters my room with a steaming bowl of delicious-smelling chili and a glass of chocolate milk. "Here. Eat this." He hands me the bowl and sets my milk on the nightstand.

"I'm sorry I opened my mouth down there. I know I'm supposed to keep the peace. I can't believe him."

"Have you talked to Sawyer today? I know you get grouchy when you miss his calls."

"He hasn't called in over a week. He's on a fishing trip with his dad." I speak in between bites of chili.

"When he calls, you can tell him you'll be in Mission Valley before the end of the month. For good." Jubal sits on my bed wearing the biggest smile.

I want to jump up and down. I want to dance around and do cartwheels. But there is a deep-seeded fear that it'll never really happen. "That's great, Jubal."

"Remember when I left the other day? I met my brother. I gave him the money for the garage. It's for real. I was going to wait to tell you until you stopped bumping into walls … but I can't hold it in any longer." Jubal laughs at me.

The picture in my head is beautiful: Jubal is changing the oil on a customer's car. The radio is playing some old country station and he is singing along. I come in to the garage to show him the 'A' on my accounting exam. He makes a bigger deal than it deserves, but I love it. I tell him about Jillian, the girl that sits next to me in class. Her breath is horrible and she loves to gossip so she's constantly leaning in to whisper about the latest juicy topic. We are truly happy.

Jubal waves a hand in front of my face, bringing my attention back to him. "Are you okay?"

"Okay? I'm so excited. The only thing stopping me from doing back flips is this bowl of chili." It's not the only thing but I don't want to worry him with the spinning walls and dancing black spots I see when I close my eyes.

"That's a sight to see, I'm sure. You are as graceful as a bull in a china shop." I look at him slightly confused. "You know? A bull running around breaking dishes in a fancy china shop?"

I laugh but the dancing black spots and dizziness make me stop. It's getting better … the spots used to be constant. Dr. Feldman told me the symptoms might linger on for a long time to come. It's like a daily reminder of what living a stupid life will get me. "I didn't know what you meant. I pictured Mr. Wong's store with a bull inside."

~~~~~~~~~~

"Well, It's all set. I told Mikus we'll be gone within the month. He is back on the dope. I'm sure you noticed. He asked if we'd run it through the garage. He doesn't get it. This is the life he wants. It's not just getting by for him."

"No shit? I can't believe you finally see it. I've been telling you this for a long time now," I say, laying my head back on the pillow.

"You're smarter than me. I get it. Now, it's time for you to stay put and get well. Dr. Feldman will be by next week to check on you and maybe get you out of that stinky cast." Jubal stands and takes the empty chili bowl with him.

I lie there staring at the ceiling trying to bring back the beautiful picture of our lives. Jubal will be busy doing what he loves. I'll be a high school graduate taking college courses. Together, we will run JV's Garage. I'm beyond excited to tell Sawyer. I fall asleep with these glorious images in my head, hoping they follow me into my dreams.

"Ian... Ian, wake up." Sawyer moves the hair from my face. "Ian..."

"I'm up, I'm up." I struggle to open my eyes but I'm so tired.

"Why did you lie to me? Did you think I wouldn't understand? Did you think my love was conditional? How can I trust you? I came to say goodbye. I can't pretend that you'll ever change. You'll always be a lowlife wannabe thug." Sawyer kisses me softly. "You are nothing but a liar. I loved you, Ian. I really did." Sawyer kisses me again, this time even harder. He leans down and bites me on my chest. I try to fight but I can't move.

"I'm sorry. I'm so sorry. Please let me explain. Don't hurt me. Don't hurt me."

"Ian!" Jubal opens the door and is at my side sitting me up, pulling me into his arms. "Ian. It's okay. Wake up."

"Jubal! I'm bad. I deserve everything that happens to me. I'm bad. My parents told me I was bad. Sawyer told me too." I'm sobbing into Jubal's chest.

"It was just a dream, Ian. It's not real. You're not bad." Jubal holds me close, petting my hair. "I'll get you something to drink."

"No! Please don't leave me."

"I'm just going to get a glass of water. I'll be right back."

Jubal turns the hall light on, leaving my room dark. I sit up and pull all of the extra pillows behind me. I don't want to fall back asleep.

"Here. Take these." Jubal hands me two Valium pills, prescribed by Dr. Feldman.

I take the pills and finish the glass of water. I am more oriented now but still highly upset. "It's either rats or my loved ones telling me they are leaving me. I can't take it. I'm sorry for the bad things I've done."

"It's just bad dreams. They'll pass. Think of the good things. Like, tomorrow we will start packing. I'm going to start moving our stuff to the garage."

"You are? When are we going?"

"You won't be going. You're getting better but you're not well enough to travel. I'll give your love to Jim and Sawyer. Lie back down and close your eyes."

"Will you stay with me, Jubal? I'm so afraid to fall asleep."

Jubal goes to his room to get his blanket. I scoot over to give him plenty of room. I'm feeling the effects of the medication. I'm no longer thinking about what evil will meet me in slumber. I know that my best friend is next to me, protecting me from the monsters.

"Ian. Do you think we're bad?" Jubal talks barely above a whisper.

"I think we do bad things. But we try to be good."

"You've always been good. You're a good girl, Ian. Don't ever doubt that, okay?"

"Okay, Jubal. You're good too, huh?" By now the Valium has fully kicked in, pulling me unwillingly into sweet dreamless sleep.

When I open my eyes I hear the guys outside. I carefully make my way to the window. Mikus is helping Jubal load the trailer. I can't make out what they're saying, and honestly don't care. I go into the kitchen. Nothing sounds good, but I need food to take my medication. I settle on instant oatmeal and toast.

I make a hot bath with lots of bubbles. I know Jubal won't let me help, so I might as well enjoy the day. Spending another day locked in my bedroom is not an option.

"Ian. You okay?" Jubal knocks on the door.

"Yep. I'm taking a bubble bath. Calgon! Take me away!"

"I'm heading out. I'll see you later tonight. Don't do anything but rest!"

"I'm going to watch a lot of TV and drink massive amounts of chocolate milk," I say in a bored monotone voice.

Jubal laughs his way down the hall. "You drink more chocolate milk than a class full of first-graders."

I miss him the moment I hear his Blazer drive away from the house. The thought of getting out of the tub is unappealing, so I keep adding hot water to the tub until I'm completely wrinkled except the cast on my left forearm. Jubal is right … it is stinky.

I dry off and pull on my robe before twisting my long hair up into a towel. I really think it's time for a new style. I open the door a crack and make sure the coast is clear before stepping across the hall into my bedroom. I wonder if Mikus went with Jubal. I doubt it.

I enjoy the quiet house for hours. I watch some fabulous television and work on a letter to Sawyer. I miss him. I love that he's close with his parents. Do they really like me or are they just polite? Patty really went out of her way to make me feel special. I think I'll pick up some pretty fingernail polish when I get out of this prison cell of a room.

After folding the laundry and changing the sheets on my bed, I take my medicine and crawl under the covers. I'm on the verge of falling asleep when I hear Mikus pull up on his motorcycle. I walk to the window to see if he's alone or if he's brought one of his hookers home with him. He's alone.

He pulls off his helmet and runs his fingers through his wild red hair. He's pacing like a crazy person. I lock my bedroom door and get back to the window. He's arguing with himself. I'm half-amused. He reaches in his saddlebag and pulls something out. I squint to see it clearly.

He turns to face the house so I duck out of sight. I'm afraid he may have seen me. I don't dare check. I crawl into bed staring at the ceiling. I think the medication is messing with my head. I swear he just pulled my backpack from his saddlebag.

Does that mean he found the punks that hurt me? Did he kill them? My body trembles with fear. I can't ask him about it. I'll just wait for Jubal. He can find out.

"Ian?" Mikus knocks on my door. He did see me.

"What, Mikus?" I ask in my best *I'm sleeping* voice.

"I brought you a burger from that place you like."

I don't know where the strength comes from but I crawl out of bed and pause before unlocking my door. Mikus has clearly neglected to smooth his hair. His unshaven face makes him look scarier than usual.

"Thank you, Mikus." I reach for the burger, forcing my hand to be still.

"Were you sleeping?" Mikus' head twitches to the right several times. "I didn't mean to wake you."

Shit. He knows. The Valium is kicking in, though. Maybe I can pull this off. "Yeah. The meds make me so tired. I had a headache earlier so I took a pain pill. They knock me out."

Mikus stands there and stares at me for a few seconds before letting go of the food. "Try to get some sleep." His eyes are wild and vacant.

"Thanks for the burger." I close the door and lock it. The meds really are kicking in. I can hardly see straight. I clumsily crawl into bed. There is no way I'm eating that burger.

I've got to get out to the garage and find my backpack. Maybe my eyes have been playing tricks on me. I can't ask Mikus about it. I fight off sleep, but only for a few moments.

Jubal comes into my room but I'm so tired I don't wake fully. He covers me up and pets my head for a few minutes before leaving. I want him to sit with me so I can tell him about the pack. Did I see my pack? Did I dream about a backpack?

The second my eyes open, I turn to see a wrapped burger on my nightstand. Disappointment washes over me. It wasn't a dream. I stand and get dressed. After brushing my tangled hair, I make my way into the kitchen.

"Morning, Jubal." I yawn.

"You must've been exhausted. Mikus said you went to sleep yesterday afternoon. You didn't even eat the burger he brought you."

"Oh, yeah. I was pretty tired. Did you get the stuff offloaded okay?"

"Yes. Jim brought Ricky and Marcus with him. He had them clean the shop out. Like, really clean it. They put down cement paint. It looks so great! I can't wait for you to see it." Jubal flips the egg high into the air, catching it without looking.

"Show off." Mikus appears, rubbing his forehead. He walks straight to the fridge for a beer.

"Hey, Mikus. Thanks again for the burger. I fell asleep before I could eat it. I'm sorry."

"Don't mention it."

"I've been meaning to ask you something. Was Julio really pissed about the money from that night?"

Mikus takes his time chugging the beer. He finishes with a loud belch. "He was. I tried to track them little pricks down, but they're vapor. I had to do a few different jobs for him to make up for it. Don't worry about it."

Maybe I was imagining seeing the pack. I feel so confused. It's his fault. He's always been such a jerk to me. It's only natural for me not to trust him.

"Jubal, are you taking another load today?" Mikus grabs a second beer.

"Yep. Those guys were on it yesterday, man. We set up the compressors and fixed the lift after offloading everything. That place is lookin' *all that*. You wanna come with today?"

Mikus shakes his head while finishing off his second beer. "I have to go to Reno. Julio still has me doing his bitch work." He directs the last sentence to me.

Chapter Eighteen

"Hold still," Dr. Feldman orders.

"I can't. I want out of this thing so bad!"

"Do you want me to cut the cast off or your arm? I said... hold still." He looks over his glasses and gives me a wink.

My left arm is a soggy wrinkly mess. "Why is it so small?" I'm disgusted.

"It's atrophy. It will return to normal in no time. The smell, however, will last forever."

He thinks he is the funniest thing ever. I thank Dr. Feldman and tell Jubal to stop laughing, then head straight for the shower. I scrub my arm at least ten times. It feels amazing to wash myself with both hands.

I get out of the shower and apply a special lotion Dr. Feldman left for me. He said I should expect to see peeling in a couple of days. The lotion will help protect my skin from breaking down.

It's hard not to think about that night in the motel room. Still, I don't know why pieces are missing. I play it in my head, trying to connect the dots. I remember Jimmy stopping me from leaving. He wanted me to stay and party. I don't remember doing anything to piss him off. I don't know why he hurt me. Maybe with the cast off and the bruises all but gone, I can move on and not think about it every day of my life.

Jubal has to work for Sylvia tonight. He asks me if I want to go, but Reno is the last place I want to be. He reminds me to lock up tight after they leave. Julio has Mikus on a short leash these days. I don't mind. He's back to doing more dope than he sells. He's mean to me when he's high, and meaner when he's coming down.

I heat up some leftover meatloaf and mashed potatoes and wrap up in Jubal's recliner. The one in his bedroom is more comfy but the big television is down here in the living room. I have the large comforter from my bed to keep me warm and an enormous glass of chocolate milk. I click on the TV just as the phone rings.

"Hello?"

"Hey, beautiful. I've missed hearing your voice." Sawyer sounds exhausted.

"Sawyer! I have some news."

"Let's hear it."

"Jubal has been moving our stuff to the garage. We'll be there in a few days. For good!"

"Seriously? Holy shit! I've been waiting to hear those words for so long now!"

"I know. I'm still recovering from my concussion but I got the cast off. You should see my arm. It looks all wrinkly and so much smaller than my right arm."

"Do you want me to drive down and help with anything? I'm taking some time off. This last trip to the new store in Idaho was rough. But after a good night's sleep in my own bed, I'll be ready to go bright and early."

"Thanks, Sawyer. But I'm pretty sure Jubal's got it under control. You just rest up because you owe me a day on the lake. It's been so long since we've actually spent time together, I almost don't remember what you look like." I close my eyes and picture his face as he talks to me.

"I remember you. Your long blonde hair, and big brown eyes… your big, kissable lips and those cute freckles on your nose. I will never forget you."

"Sawyer, you are so sweet. I can't believe its finally happening. Are you sure you're ready to have me around full time?" I hold my breath waiting for his answer.

"I guess it's too late to back out now…" Sawyer

half-laughs, half-yawns.

"I'll let you go, Sawyer. I can tell you're tired. Tell your folks hi for me, okay?"

"Good night, Ian."

Good night, Sawyer."

It's not long after I hang up that I'm falling asleep. I don't want to fall asleep down here. I force myself upstairs and lock myself in my room, although the thing I'm most afraid of is another nightmare. I take two Valium and pray for a dreamless night.

Jubal is knocking on my door. "Wake up, sleepyhead. I'm making your favorite."

"You sure do know how to start a day off right!" I throw on some sweats and pull my messy hair into a pony before stepping into the kitchen, thankful for pure uninterrupted sleep.

"Where's Mikus? Is he sleeping?" I whisper.

"No. He had to stay in Reno. Something is very wrong with him. He won't talk to me about it. Maybe he's upset that I'm leaving. He's gotta be thrilled that you're out of here, though!"

We both get a good laugh at his joke. We head out to the garage. He must see that I'm feeling better or he'd order me back to bed. He boxes up random extension cords and power tools. I offer to push the broom but he tells me to spread the floor sweep and he'll push the broom.

"You just got out of the cast yesterday!" Jubal shakes his head.

I grab the bucket of floor sweep and sprinkle it on the grease-stained concrete floor. I have been warned so often to stay away from Mikus' toolboxes, I never realized how much crap he's collected. I turn around to say something to Jubal, bumping a workbench and

159

sending a crowbar to the floor. It makes such a loud sound I'm actually worried Mikus will spontaneously appear to yell at me for touching his stuff. I kneel down to pick up the crowbar when I see it.

The bright purple strap of my backpack is playing peek-a-boo from under a cabinet. I'm afraid I might shatter into a million pieces. Mikus said he couldn't track them down. They were vapor. Seeing the backpack sends me back to the motel. Jimmy is hollering at Wilson. I can hear it clearly now. "*Mikus told you to beat her up and scare her a little bit.*"

"Ian? Are you okay?"

"No. I feel sick. Can you help me to my room? I guess I'm not feeling as well as I thought." I'm on the verge of screaming my lungs out. I don't know where to start. Would he even believe me?

Jubal guides me towards my room. I stumble into the bathroom just in time to crouch down in front of the toilet before I vomit. I must scare Jubal, because he wants to call Dr. Feldman.

"No. I'm okay. I just got dizzy or something."

Mikus put on such an act. I even thanked him for saving me. My head is spinning. I remember everything that happened. I remember being struck in the back of the head, with an empty Jack Daniels bottle. I remember pleading to Wilson for help as Jimmy enjoyed my cries of pain. All of it was on Mikus' orders. I vomit again.

"I'm calling Dr. Feldman." Jubal leaves me kneeling on the floor before I can beg him not to.

When he returns he hands me a wet washcloth. With one swoop I'm in his arms and he's carrying me to my bed. He takes my sweats off and helps me into my nightshirt. I'm full-on sobbing and no matter how badly I try to stop, I can't.

Dr. Feldman tells Jubal to give me more Valium and sit with me until he arrives. Jubal pulls me into his arms and pets me, repeating the words he spoke that night. "It's okay. I've got you. I've got you."

It's dark out when Dr. Feldman arrives. He takes my temperature, checks my pulse and questions me. He diagnoses me with post-concussion syndrome. It is very common to have bouts of anxiety, fear and depression after traumatic events. I do not tell them about Mikus.

The Valium starts to wear off and I begin to dry heave and hyperventilate. Dr. Feldman offers an injection but I panic at his words so he decides against it. He gives Jubal a bottle of stronger sedatives with instructions on how much to give me.

I'm fading into darkness. I hear their voices but they are too muffled. I fight off sleep. I can't face the rats in my dreams. I know they'll be there, and this time they'll be joined by Mikus. I am pulled into unconsciousness unwillingly and am greeted by my enemies.

"We've been waiting for you." Wilson and Jimmy speak in unison, then begin snorting endless lines of cocaine with their rat-like faces.

The floor is covered in broken glass, empty beer cans and rotting food. I stand frozen to the spot.

"I tried to find them but they were vapor." Mikus keeps repeating the lie. "I was, however, able to find someone even better... your father." Mikus points a thick freckled finger at the darkened corner.

My father steps into the light. His booted feet walk across the green floral linoleum of our kitchen. His hands clench into fists. He walks towards me. His face isn't human or rat. He opens his mouth but there is no tongue or any teeth, just a black hole. Black holes for eyes. Black holes for nostrils. He orders me to come to him. I do not move. He reminds me what happens when I disrespect him like a mutt dog would.

The links clink together as he lifts the long length of chain and walks towards me to wrap around my neck. A bad dog gets treated like a bad dog. A chained dog cannot run. A chained dog can only cry out in agony from the beating it deserves. I am not a dog. I am not a dog. I tell myself over and over ... I am not a dog.

Mikus sits there like a student finally learning how to work a math problem. His eyes light up with pure joy, as this type of torture has never entered his mind. The attention only makes my father more animated in his teaching. I struggle to get away from the chain link noose. I close my eyes wishing it away. When I open them I see no Mikus, no rats or my father. I see Sawyer. He walks hand in hand with a beautiful red-haired girl. They smile and laugh as they pass right by me. I call out to him in vain.

I scream as loud as my lungs will allow. I kick and punch and run. Nothing happens. I end up where I started. I crumple to the floor in a defeated mess, willing Jubal to save me. My eyes closed tight, I repeat his name over and over. I hear his footsteps. The sounds aren't getting louder. They are fading. He is leaving me. No words are spoken. He just leaves. I give up. I lie there focusing on slowing my breaths. Slower. Slower.

A hand touches my shoulder. I open my eyes and see... me. She waves a hand and beckons me to follow. I walk through uneven ground and around potholes. There's a light up ahead. The closer I get, the brighter the light, until it is so bright my eyes are squinting. I wonder if I'm dead. But my eyes adjust and I see that the bright light is the sun reflecting off the lake. I'm standing *on the beach behind the garage. The sun is warm on my face. The sand between my toes tickles. The sign in front of the garage is beautiful: JV's Garage. I suddenly feel happy. Relaxed. Peaceful.*

I sit up in bed. Jubal is next to me half covered by a blanket that is too small for his enormous body. His snoring must've woken me. The sun has been up for a while. I probably kept Jubal up for most of the night. I decide to let him sleep.

I grab a pen and a notebook from my nightstand and begin jotting down the details of my dream. I can't wait for Jubal to wake up so I can tell him about it. Reality fills my head, after the dream is put on paper. Mikus did this to me. I can't wait until I never have to see him again.

"Morning. How'd you sleep?"

"Jubal! I'm so sorry. I can't believe I freaked out like that."

"It's not like you decided to have a meltdown. Dr. Feldman said it's normal. I felt bad that I couldn't calm you down. Do you know why it happened?" Jubal stretches his cramped limbs.

"I started to have flashes of that night." Afraid of his reaction, I leave it at that.

"Ian, I'm really sorry. Maybe when we move into our new place you'll start to feel better."

Jubal gets up to take a leak. I wonder if I can get out to the garage before he's finished in the bathroom. I need to get the backpack. I climb out of bed and look out the window just in time to see Mikus pulling into the garage. Suddenly, my fear is replaced with anger. I'm not afraid of Mikus. He's a coward.

Jubal comes in to ask me if I'd like something to eat. "What's wrong? You're trembling. Are you okay?"

"I'm okay. I'm cold." I lie.

We go downstairs where we meet Mikus in the kitchen. I stare at the floor. I'm afraid if I look at him I'll scratch his face off. I need to figure things out in my head, first.

"What's up with the garage? There's floor sweep all over the place." Mikus throws his leather on the hook and puts a six-pack in the fridge.

"Ian was helping me clean up but she got dizzy." I'm thankful for Jubal's vague answer.

"Something made me sick." I force my eyes to make contact with his.

Mikus looks to the garage and back at me. "Maybe the fumes got to ya."

"Maybe."

Chapter Nineteen

Today is the day. I throw the last of my clothes into a cardboard box and carry it downstairs. I woke with the perfect plan. I'm going to get the backpack from the garage and confront Mikus with Jubal standing right there. He can explain it to both of us.

"I told you to let me know when you were finished packing so you wouldn't carry it." Jubal is sitting at the table eating cereal, pointing at me with his spoon.

"I told you I'm fine! We are out of here. That makes everything better." I smile until I see Mikus walk in the kitchen door, letting the screen slam behind him.

He looks like a wounded animal. His eyes are looking more skeletal every day. I hope this is the last day I'll ever have to see him. I walk by him without a word. My pulse quickens with each step closer to the garage. I put the box in the back seat of my car and glance over my shoulder, checking to see if the coast is clear.

I walk to the front of the car and kneel down to pull the backpack from under the cabinet. There is nothing there but dust and floor sweep. I stand and immediately turn, expecting to see Mikus standing there, but I'm alone.

My feet are moving swiftly towards the screen door. I don't care if I have the backpack or not. He's going to have to face what he did. I take a deep breath and reach for the handle when I hear them.

"I need you to get help, man. I've only had a handful of people in this life who mean anything to me and you are one of them. I love you, brother. It kills me to see you like this." Jubal is talking in a stern voice, pleading with Mikus.

"I'm a fuck up. I don't think there's hope for me,

man. I'm tired of this life." Mikus is standing with his back to the door.

"I don't know what I'd do if you weren't in my life. Do you remember what you said to me when I stole from you? You said there wasn't anything I could do to make you turn your back on me. Well, I'm telling you the same thing."

My plan is ruined. I can't make Jubal choose between us. I walk to the front porch and sit on the step. I can't forget what happened to me and I won't forgive him. I will never forgive him.

"Ian?" Jubal is calling out my name from the garage.

"Hey." I wipe the tears from my cheeks and meet him by his Blazer.

"I have to make a quick trip to Reno before I can go to Mission Valley. Do you want to go ahead of me and I'll meet you?"

"Is Mikus going with you?"

"Yeah, but he's waiting for a call first."

"I'll wait for you. I want us to go together."

"Are you okay?"

Those three words make me laugh. I don't know if I'll ever be okay. "I'll be okay when we are far away from this place."

We go inside to find Mikus snorting a line in the living room. He looks at Jubal, ignoring my presence. "I need a little bump for the ride."

"Ian's gonna stay here. Did you get your call?"

"I'll call him." He taps the rolled up dollar bill on the mirror and wipes the residual powder on his gums.

"I'm out, man. I need to make this a quick trip. Jim's expecting us around nine."

Jubal throws on his leather and walks to the

kitchen door. Mikus follows him into the kitchen, picking up the telephone. I want to wrap the cord around his stupid neck.

"Be safe, Jubal." I give him a grin.

Mikus talks into the phone with crazy hand gestures like the person on the other end can see him. "I know, Julio. I got it."

Jubal looks at me and smiles. "I'll be back soon as I can. I can already taste Jim's chili." His laugh follows him outside.

I stand by the screen door watching him drive away. There is a pit in my stomach. I now know I can never tell him what Mikus did. Jubal may be a big strong black man, but he's broken just like I am. I can't hurt him. I won't hurt him.

The room is silent. I turn to see Mikus holding the phone in his hand, a wicked smile on his face.

"Yeah, Julio. She still thinks I'm really talking on the phone. But we know better." He keeps his eyes on me as he hangs the receiver back on the wall.

I push the screen open but he lunges at me, grabbing a handful of my hair. He digs his fingers into my arm, squeezing it like a vise. "Come here, little girl."

"Jubal trusted you!" I scream.

"Shut up! Don't you talk to me about Jubal—you turned him against me." He drags me into the living room, throwing me to the floor. He opens the end table cabinet and tosses the bright backpack into my lap. "Is this what you've been looking for? You think I'm stupid?"

I stand slowly. "I'm sorry, Mikus. I am. I won't tell. I promise."

He slaps me with the back of his hand. My world spins into a blurry mess. I wobble to my knees. I taste blood. Mikus stands above me spewing hateful words with each slap and kick he delivers.

My face is on the floor. I'm too dizzy to move. Mikus is pacing back and forth, still spitting out words of hate. My finger tickles the brown carpet fibers, as I fight to hold onto consciousness. I see the blade he uses to make the bindles out of magazine pages under the coffee table. I move slowly and clumsily for it, stopping when I think he's watching. I wrap my fingers around the blade and turn, waving it wildly in his direction.

"Stupid little girl." He laughs at my attempt as he slowly cocks his 9-mm.

I close my eyes. I picture the faces of the ones I love. Jubal. Jim. Sawyer. I drop the blade and accept my fate. "I'm not a dog." The words come out in a whisper. I know I've done bad things, but I am not a bad person.

"I should've had them kill you."

There is a loud bang. I wait for the pain of the bullet wound, but feel nothing. I open my eyes and see Jubal and Mikus wrestling. It's easy for Jubal to gain control over Mikus' emaciated body. There's a bullet hole in the wall above the window.

"What the fuck is wrong with you? She's just a kid!" Jubal takes the clip from the gun and tosses the gun at Mikus' feet. "You told them punks to do that? You even played the concerned friend perfectly. It was *your* idea to take her to Dr. Feldman."

"Jubal. I'm sorry." I can't stop the room from spinning. I feel a wave of nausea come over me.

"Mikus! Do you see what you've done to her?" He's screaming his question. "Look at her! You did this! She's just a kid!" Jubal kneels down to help me up.

Mikus sits on the floor leaning against the wall. His shaking hands are folded over his bent knees.

"Why did you come back?" I grip his arm trying to steady myself.

"I figured Sylvia could wait. I've made you wait long enough to get out of here. I'm glad I did." Anger still pulses through his veins, and I can feel it as I grip onto him.

"Me too." I smile.

There's a sudden pounding on the front door. Jubal looks at Mikus, who grabs for his gun and clip. He fumbles trying to get the two pieces into one. "Get out of here, Jubal."

"What do you mean, get out of here? Who's out there?" Jubal is still trying to get me to my feet.

I take a deep breath and force myself on steady feet. Jubal's tone is one of fear. He asks Mikus again.

"It's Julio, or Julio's lackeys. I fucked up bad this time!" Mikus isn't scared. His eyes are wild and he's ready for a fight. "Yeah, it's Julio and two of his boys." Mikus peeks through the side of the curtain.

The pounding at the door is louder. "Mikus! We know you're in there. Get your ass out here!"

"Can you walk?" Jubal has both my arms holding me upright. His nose almost touches mine. "I need you to walk."

"I can walk." I think I can walk, anyway. Jubal leads me to the back of the house.

We step into the laundry room and hear the living room window shatter. We freeze, waiting to hear what's happening.

"Julio! I told you, we can work this out, man!" Mikus calls out.

"Ian. Can you drive?" Jubal is talking fast. "I need you to sneak to the garage and get to Jim's. I'll be there as soon as I clean up his fucking mess."

169

"No! I …"

"Please, Ian!" He peeks out the laundry room door to see if it's clear. "Go!"

I'm walking on tiptoes to the garage. The closer I get to the front of the house the more I can hear. Julio wants his dope and his money. Mikus is trying to convince him he's got a plan. I hear another gunshot. I turn my head to make sure I'm not a target. The men are standing by a Cadillac, laughing. The shot appears to have been a warning shot, fired straight up in the air.

Julio sees me. I stop in my tracks. He gives a little nod with his head. I run to my car, fire up the engine and drive. I roll my window down hoping the fresh air will help with the nausea. It doesn't. I pull over on the side of the road and throw up. I turn the car around and head back to the ranch only to turn around again. I can't make things harder for Jubal right now.

"*Why?*" I'm shouting to the heavens. Tears are streaming down my cheeks. I reach for the glove box and pull out a napkin. I wipe my cheeks and dab the corners of my bloody mouth. The metallic taste is stuck in my mouth. The only thing I have to drink is a warm can of Dr. Pepper. I suck in a mouthful of soda, swishing it around my mouth before spitting it out the window.

I drive into Mission Valley and fear overwhelms me. I pull into the first gas station I see. I park by the restrooms and step inside, thankful for the vacancy. The mirror is scratched and warped but I can see my eye is black and my lip and cheek are swollen. I rinse the blood from my mouth and wash it from my hair.

When I pull up to Jim's I'm surprised when he meets me at the porch. He hugs me softly and helps me inside. I choke back tears but I'm unable to stop my lip from quivering. Sawyer is in the kitchen pouring me some hot tea.

"Jubal called and let me know you were on your way. He said you've been hurt but didn't have time to give details. I can see you're hurt so I'm not going to push you tonight, but you better believe I'll be expecting answers tomorrow."

"I need to take my medicine. My head hurts but I couldn't take anything because I had to drive." I'm embarrassed they are looking at me like I'm a wounded bird.

"I was here when Jubal called. We've been working on a project. I had to stay to make sure you were okay. I'm going to leave so you can get some rest. I'll come by tomorrow to check on you." Sawyer kisses the top of my head then kneels down so he can look me in the eyes. "I love you."

"I love you, too. I'm glad you're here. Do you have to go?" I wipe the tear from his cheek. "I need to shower. Can you help me?"

Sawyer's eyes are almost as wide as Jim's. "I don't think that's a good idea." Sawyer blushes.

"I need somebody's help. I have dried blood all over and I stink of vomit." I set the mug on the table and stand up on wobbly legs.

Jim looks at Sawyer with an "I'm not doing it" look. "Sawyer, you know where the towels are."

Sawyer walks me upstairs to the bathroom. He pulls two fresh towels from the closet. "Come here."

With shaky hands, Sawyer lifts the baggy sweatshirt over my head. "Holy shit." His hands cup his face.

"It looks worse than it feels. I promise." I am bruised all over my trunk and arms. I'm sure my legs will be the same. I'm able to slide my pants off without assistance.

Sawyer turns on the water, adjusting it to the perfect temperature, checking it several times with his hand. He stands in front of me with tears threatening to spill down his face. "I'm afraid to touch you."

"Don't be afraid. I'm okay. I need you to help me wash my hair and make sure I don't fall." I smile.

Sawyer undresses and I realize that this isn't Jubal helping me bathe. It is my boyfriend. I've never seen him naked before. I'm not embarrassed. It's not like this is a sexy moment—far from it. He helps me into the tub and the water feels amazing. Sawyer takes the bar of soap and washes my back and arms. I turn to face him. He has a look of such sadness in his eyes.

"Your body is covered in bruises, Ian. I can't even imagine what you've been through." He pulls me in to his chest and holds me. He doesn't push for information. He just holds me.

"I'm sorry our first shower has to be like this. We shouldn't be crying and washing vomit out of my hair." I smile.

Sawyer helps me wash where I can't reach. I wash the places I can. I'm thankful the bite mark has healed enough to look like another bruise. After my hair rinses clean he leans down and kisses me softly on the mouth. It's like a kiss in a warm summer rain. I can feel my body relax. The tension I've held onto since the night in the motel is released, and I feel safe in his arms.

We step out of the shower, and Sawyer helps me dry off and brush out my hair. He gets dressed while I'm wrapped in a towel. I have clothes in my room. Sawyer helps me dress in sweats and the Freedom Farms t-shirt.

Jim comes upstairs with my bag and a glass of water. I swallow the pills and hope they take effect quickly. Jim asks if there's anything else he can get for me before going to bed. I ask him if it'll be okay for Sawyer to stay.

"Of course he can stay. I'm damn glad he's here. It's been a rough night. I'll see you in the morning." Jim gives me an I-don't-want-to-break-you hug and pats Sawyer on the shoulder.

I get in bed, feeling the pull of sleep. I scoot over making room for Sawyer. He slides in after me and snuggles me in close. "I'm glad you're here. Thank you for not asking a million questions. And thank you for helping me shower."

"I've pictured us taking a shower together. It went nothing like that." He giggles.

"Maybe we can try again sometime." I close my eyes and picture his naked body so close to mine.

Sawyer kisses the top of my head. "Can I ask you something?"

"Yeah." My voice is growing tired.

"Will you love me forever?"

"Yeah." I smile and take this feeling with me to my dreams.

Chapter Twenty

I wake and immediately feel the aches and pains from yesterday. Sawyer is still holding me. I could stay here forever ... but I have to see if Jubal's here yet. The slightest movement wakes Sawyer.

"Good morning, Ian." He pulls me in for a tender hug.

"Morning. Let's go downstairs and get some breakfast. I'm so hungry."

Sawyer laughs at my excitement for food. "I love how you are not girly. You eat what you want to eat and say what you want. You're fearless."

I turn to see whom he is talking to. "*What*? I'm girly!" I throw my pillow at him.

"Well, at least you throw like a girl." Sawyer holds out a hand to help me out of bed.

Jim is in the kitchen drinking his coffee. Fancy is by his side. I see another dog with her.

"Is that CJ?" I squat on the floor and pull her into my arms. "I thought you homed all of them. Did they not want her?" A look of worry floods my face.

"Everyone wanted her. But I told them she was taken. She belongs to you, Ian." Jim has an enormous smile on his hairy face.

I would cry if I weren't so happy. CJ is giving me kisses. "She remembers me."

"Jim's been waiting for you to get here. I wasn't sure he'd be able to keep her a secret much longer." Sawyer fixes two cups of coffee and sits at the table.

"Is Jubal here?" I feel a pang of guilt for being distracted by puppy love.

"Nope. I'm guessing things with Mikus ran late into the night. He said Mikus really messed things up this time. I'm also guessing Mikus is the one behind your bruises." Jim sips his coffee, looking at me to confirm his suspicions.

"I'm okay. I've had worse." I try to play it off.

"We've seen you worse. Not too long ago." This time it's Sawyer who pipes in.

"Come on, guys. I'm okay. I know you want answers but I can't give them to you. Not now. I promise when Jubal gets here we'll explain everything." I turn my attention back to CJ.

"Somebody mentioned chili omelets." Sawyer tries to relax the mood.

"I'm on it!" I pat CJ's cute block-shaped head, letting her kiss me one more time.

I open the fridge and collect eggs, onion, chili, cheese, and butter. I am on a mission to create the most delicious breakfast ever. Jim's even made his homemade biscuits. They are amazing. I pick one apart and munch on it while cooking. "See, Sawyer? I'm girly," I say with a mouth full of biscuit.

We sit at the table eating and drinking coffee and sharing small talk. I know they want answers but I can't go there. I'm afraid of how they'll see me. Small talk is best. "Where are the guys, Jim?"

"They're bringing some cattle over from Montana. They'll be gone a few more days." Jim glances at the clock for the fifth time. He doesn't think I notice.

Sawyer offers to clean the dishes. I don't argue. I take some Tylenol to get the pounding in my head to stop.

"I'm going to check on Lulu. Would you like to help me feed her?" Jim stands with a stretch and another glance at the clock.

"I'd love to. I can't wait until I feel strong enough to ride." The thought of riding her now makes me want to grab the wall to steady myself. Stupid concussion. Stupid Mikus.

We tend to the animals. Jim is kind and treats them with love. I'm always amazed at his warmth. I wonder how two broken boys like Jubal and Jim were able to grow into such loving men. I'm thankful for both of them.

"I'm low on feed for the chickens. I think I'll ask Sawyer to run into town." Jim closes the gate behind us.

I ask Jim for a pair of sunglasses so I can go into town with Sawyer. The question puts a frown on both of their faces. "I can always tell people I'm really bad at makeup!" I laugh. The guys do not.

The drive into town is gorgeous. The cool air is refreshing. I sit close to Sawyer, resting my hand on his leg.

"Ian. I need to know something." Sawyer grips the steering wheel.

"Okay." I take a breath in anticipation.

"Did you sneak a peek in the shower?" Sawyer looks at me, trying hard to keep a straight face.

I can't help the color that rushes to my cheeks. "Oh my gosh! You did not just ask me that!" I slap his leg.

We walk through the store hand in hand. Sawyer introduces me to Louise and Susan Bradford, sisters that spend their time split between church and their farm. I can tell they find it very rude of me to have sunglasses on inside. I speak very politely to them and fib about having pink eye. This helps, and they add me to their prayer list after giving me several home remedies.

"Stop introducing me to people or I'm going to take these shades off and tell people you beat up my face!" I squeeze Sawyer's hand tightly.

"You wouldn't dare!" He drops my hand and gives me a mischievous grin.

"Don't do it. Don't!" It's too late. Sawyer puts his hands out like the boogie monster and chases me down the aisle.

I'm giggling and snorting while grabbing random things off the shelves and tossing them at him. It doesn't last very long. I'm winded quickly.

"I'm sorry." Sawyer grows serious.

"It's okay. I'm just a little out of shape."

We walk upstairs where he shares a large office with his father. There are pictures of him and his parents on the walls. His father's desk has a framed photo of his wedding day. Sawyer has a picture of me on his desk. It's from my first barbecue at Jim's.

"I didn't know this was taken. What a great day."

"Yeah. I loved your smile the first time I saw it."

The bathroom door opens and Steve greets us cheerfully. "This is a nice surprise! How are you, Ian? I didn't expect you two."

"Jim asked me to pick up some feed."

"How's your project coming along?" He raises his eyebrows.

"Good. Almost finished." Sawyer speaks without much movement of his lips.

"Am I missing something? What project?"

"Don't you worry about it, missy." Sawyer winks at me. "We better get back. I wanted to stop in before we left. Love you, Dad."

"It was nice to see you, Steve. Tell Patty I say hello," I add to Sawyer's goodbye.

"I will. She'll be expecting you over soon." Steve waves in farewell.

Sawyer takes my hand again and leads the way to

the chicken feed. We pass all types of barrels, bags and crates of all kinds of animal feed. It actually smells horrible. Sawyer throws a bag on his shoulder. He is so handsome. I notice the definition in his arms and wonder how I've missed that until now. I follow him to the front of the store. He says hello to the customers, but is kind and skips the introductions.

A large man in overalls and a red flannel shirt asks Sawyer about a problem with his order. Sawyer sets the bag down and excuses himself for just a moment. I stand at the front by the register watching random people come in. There's a television behind the counter showing some talk show. I watch the host adjust her large red glasses and tell the husband to keep it in his pants and take care of business at home. The audience goes wild.

I turn my attention to a shelf with rows of candy bars. I'm debating between a Payday and the Hershey's bar. Chocolate always wins. I pick a Hershey bar for me, and some Reese's Pieces for Sawyer. I see an older couple walk in. The man looks happy but his wife looks like she'll grab his cane at any moment and smack him with it. I giggle to myself.

I turn to see Sawyer walking towards me but he's not looking at me. He's staring past me with a wild look in his eyes.

I look behind me to see the talk show has been interrupted by a news report. Mikus' house is on the television. There are police and rescue vehicles all around. The reporter is interviewing a police officer in front of the bullet-ridden house. I can't hear what they're saying. I can't hear anything. Sawyer has his arms wrapped around me, holding me up. I stare at the banner running along the bottom of the screen. "THREE KILLED IN WHAT POLICE BELIEVE TO BE A

DRUG DEAL GONE WRONG."

The candy I was holding hits the floor. I look at Sawyer begging him to tell me it's not true and that Jubal's okay. He says nothing. He walks me to the truck and helps me inside. I'm rocking back and forth in the seat. "He's okay, right? Sawyer?"

"I don't know, Ian. I don't know. Let's just get back to Jim's and see what we can find out." Sawyer speeds down the road. The cool air that was refreshing an hour ago now feels like ice on my skin.

We park and run to the front door. The TV is on in the living room but Jim isn't in his chair. There's a broken glass on the floor. We find Jim in the kitchen on the telephone. I try to read his expression, but he's speaking quietly into the phone.

"Is that Jubal? Is he okay? Please!" I plead for answers.

Jim hangs up the phone and wipes his face with his handkerchief. He turns to me and Sawyer. "That was the Sheriff. Ian. Sawyer. My brother is dead."

"Don't you say that … don't you fucking say that!" I'm beating my fists into his chest. I can feel Sawyer pulling me into his arms, where I collapse in a sobbing mess.

"I'm so sorry." Sawyer helps me to the couch.

"I need to drive over and meet with the Sheriff. I have to identify the body and collect his personal belongings. Sawyer, can you stay here until I get back?"

"Of course. Are you okay to go by yourself?" Sawyer picks up the broken glass before wiping up the mess.

I realize I'm not the only one who's lost Jubal. Jim is hurting also. I go to him and hug him tight. "I'm so sorry. I'm…so…sorry." I manage to get the words out in between sobs.

Jim takes my arms from around him and forces my eyes to his. "It's okay. I'm just thankful you made it out of there." He pulls me in for a quick hug.

I go back to the couch where I curl into a ball and sob uncontrollably. Sawyer covers me with a blanket.

"Here, Ian. Take these." Jim hands me two pills from my bag.

I take the pills. "I'm sorry, Jim."

Jim nods. "Here, Sawyer. You can give her a couple more in two hours if she needs them." Jim hands the bottle to Sawyer before leaving.

I know in my head that I can't play the 'What If' game. But my heart is breaking into a million pieces and I don't know how to stop it.

"I turned the car around, Sawyer. I turned the car around." I cry into the blanket.

Sawyer sits on the floor in front of me. "What do you mean?"

"I left like he told me to. I tried to refuse but he wouldn't let me stay. I left but I pulled over and headed back. I knew he'd be pissed if I didn't listen to him so I turned the car around."

"I'm glad you did, Ian." Sawyer gets up. "I'm going to make you some tea. I'll be right in the kitchen, okay?"

"Okay, Sawyer." I close my eyes and see Jubal. The pain is excruciating. I can't breathe. I want to hear his laugh. I want to turn back time, and make him come with me, and leave Mikus to clean up his own mess. "Mikus!"

Sawyer rushes into the living room. "What?"

"This is all his fault. He knew Julio was after him. He knew Jubal wouldn't leave him. I bet this was his plan the whole time." I don't say it out loud but I hope he's dead.

"Sit up." Sawyer sits on the couch and pulls me into his arms. "Relax and let the medicine work."

I don't want to sleep. I don't want to relax. I want to scream my fucking head off until every person on the planet knows how sad I feel. How big my loss is. How my life will never be the same without Jubal.

No matter how hard I fight it, the pills always win. I can feel my mind grow fuzzy and my body heavy in Sawyer's arms.

"Sawyer. Don't let the rats get me."

"You're safe, Ian. I promise."

Chapter Twenty-One

"Jubal!" I sit up, straining to see in the darkness.

"Honey, he's not here," Jim mumbles sleepily from his recliner.

The fire Jim made is still glowing. I stare at the flames and the tears begin. Slowly, at first, then the tears turn into sobs. I grab tissues from the oak coffee table. Jim allows me to cry. We sit in the dark and mourn our loss together.

"I wanted it all to be a bad dream. I was hoping to wake up and see Jubal smiling and joking with me saying, "I told you I'd be here."

"I know what you mean. I keep looking at the clock waiting for him, too. He'd always tell me he wasn't late… 'It's called making an entrance', he'd say."

"Where's Sawyer?" I rub my swollen eyes.

"He went home. He has to fly out in the morning. He wanted to cancel but I told him I'd keep an eye on you until he gets back. Can I get you anything?"

I feel bad Jim slept in his chair for my sake. I can see by the way he struggles to get out of his chair he's exhausted and uncomfortable. "I'll get us some tea. I have to pee anyway. When I get back we can talk, okay?"

"Okay, Ian."

I flip on the bathroom light and see my bruised face in the mirror. *Is this how my life is supposed to be? Did I run away from one disaster to the next? Is there something worse than Mikus in my future?* I rinse my face with cool water and force my tears deep down inside my core. I refuse to be a whiny little victim.

I prepare the tea and return to the living room. Jim has stoked the fire. It's very calming. "I can't believe it's one-thirty in the morning. I slept for over twelve hours."

"I wouldn't call it sleep." Jim takes a sip of his

tea. "I think it's time we have that talk. I need to hear about these rats."

I don't know where to start, so I sit in silence.

Jim starts by telling me that Jubal didn't suffer. I'm thankful for that, but it still makes me cry. Jubal wanted to be cremated. Jim'll be able to bring him home once the investigation is complete.

"Did Mikus make it out of there?" I hold my breath, bracing myself for his answer.

"No. He did not. The Sheriff said he was shot in the back. He was always a coward."

"Jim, I have four months until I turn eighteen. I don't expect you to let me stay here with you, but I'm asking you if I can. But first, I will tell you everything."

"You can tell me what you're comfortable sharing with me. But there is *nothing* you can say that will make me turn my back on you. Ever. Of course, you can stay here."

"You haven't heard what I have to say yet." I take a deep breath. "I'm not actually an orphan. I ran away because my parents were abusive. I'm not lying when I say I've had worse beatings than this." I focus on the bright flames dancing in the large stone fireplace. "Jubal saw me that night on my way to sleep by the river where the homeless sleep. He called me out. He knew I was a runaway. It was fate that we found each other. The next morning he saw me in the diner. He saved my life. I trusted him immediately, although at one point I did think he was a pimp."

My story continues on, telling him how it was my idea to work for Mikus and how Jubal was against it. "Jim, I couldn't go back to my parents. I couldn't. So, I didn't think about how horrible it was that I was dealing drugs. I just knew I was able to stay with Jubal."

"I know you didn't lay a bike down. Road rash doesn't look like that. Did Mikus hurt you?"

"Sort of. Well, this time, yes. But when you came to check on me, no. This is where the rats come in. He sent me to do a drop and two guys were waiting to mess me up. Now, when I dream, that's how I see them: as rats. Anyway, Mikus just wanted to scare me a little bit. He was punishing me for taking Jubal away from him. And for stabbing him with a fork."

Jim lets out a cackle. I appreciate this more than he realizes.

I force myself to continue. "I didn't know it was Mikus who was behind it until I saw the backpack I used to carry the dope. It was very childlike with bright straps. The guys took it with them. I found it later—he hid it in the garage. I was helping Jubal and when I saw it, I had a flood of clarity from that night. I remembered what happened and what the guys said. It was more than I could handle. I debated on whether or not I should tell Jubal. I didn't even know how to tell him. I was afraid Mikus would be able to lie his way out of it. When I went back out to the garage to get the backpack it was gone. Mikus moved it. I was so pissed off I stormed back to the house but heard Jubal talking. He loved Mikus. He felt he *owed* him. I couldn't tell him after that. When Jubal left for Sylvia's, Mikus went off on me. He was more crazed than I'd ever seen him. He almost shot me." I feel my voice crack.

"Honey, you don't have to go on."

"Yes, I do. You have to know." I sip my tea and clear my throat, wiping my tears on my sleeve. "Jubal came back. He said he came back for me. He saved me—again. We were almost out of there when Julio showed up with his guys. That's when Mikus got even weirder. I swear it was like he had a death wish and that was his plan."

Jim stands to stoke the fire. His voice is fierce. "He got you out, but couldn't leave that piece of shit?"

The ability to keep my emotions intact has evaded me. I'm sobbing uncontrollably. "Why? Why didn't he leave?"

Jim sits next to me on the couch. "The same reason you never left him."

I'm shocked by his words but at the same time they give me comfort. Jubal didn't choose Mikus over me. He loved the small circle of people in his life. He couldn't turn his back on his friend.

"Jim?" My head is leaning on his shoulder.

"Huh?"

"Do you hate me?"

"Oh, no, honey. The only thing you did was what you had to do to survive."

"Can I stay with you?"

"Only if you do three things. You must study for your diploma."

"I can do that. What's the second thing?"

"You have to help out around here. You put in work just like the farm hands."

"Of course, I'll do that. What else?"

"You live every day of your life bettering yourself. No more bullshit. You walk a straight line. That's what Jubal wanted for you. That's what I want for you."

"Thank you." I hug him tight.

"You know? Sawyer is going to want some answers too." Jim gets up and nods toward the kitchen. "What're you going to do about that?"

I sit at the table while Jim dishes some ice cream.

"I can't tell him. There's no way. He's perfect. I'm still trying to figure out why he sticks with me. I don't want to lose him. If he knows the bad things I've done, he'll leave me."

"Don't be foolish. I've talked with Sawyer. He adores you. And, I'll tell you something else. Sawyer is not perfect either. There is only one perfect man and we are still waiting for Him to return. The rest of us are all flawed in one way or another."

"I'm afraid to tell him." I rinse my bowl. "And you can't tell him either."

"That is not my place to tell your business."

Jim asks if I'm okay to sleep in my room. "I'll bring the dogs in and you can take CJ with you for company."

"I'll be okay, Jim." I'm not okay. But I saw how uncomfortable he was in his recliner. "Is CJ allowed on the furniture?"

"I gave up trying to keep them off of the furniture a long time ago." Jim gives a tired laugh.

He hugs me for a long time before stoking the fire. He lets the dogs in, taking Fancy with him.

I take CJ into my room. She jumps on my bed effortlessly, and is a born cuddler. "Keep the rats away, CJ." I fall asleep as soon as my head hits the pillow.

I step into Sylvia's bar. My shoes stick to the floor as I walk to the bar. I order chocolate milk from the faceless bartender. The jukebox plays Louis Armstrong and Ella Fitzgerald in the background. The back door opens and Jubal walks in. He smiles his beautiful bright smile as he occupies the stool next to mine. "Hey. I'm sorry I'm late."

"It's okay. I knew you'd be here." I sip my milk.

"I think you'll be very happy at Jim's. He's a

great man. I always wanted to be like him when I grew up."

"*Jim wasn't mad at me. I told him everything. He still wants me to stay. He'll have me cleaning out the nasty pigpens, I bet.*" I wrinkle my nose.

Jubal laughs his wonderful joyous laugh. "He probably will. It's okay if he does. He's gonna be good for you. I wish I could've done a better job."

"*What do you mean? You showed me unconditional love. You taught me how to turn a wrench. You saved my life, more than once.*"

"*I never had a little sister until you came into my life. You brought so much happiness into my dark world. You lit a fire under my butt. I got close to my dream, too. Promise me you'll finish it, Ian. You'll be so happy there. I've sat on the beach behind the garage and watched the most beautiful sunsets.*"

"*I promise, Jubal. You'll visit when you can?*"

"*Try to stop me.*" *Jubal winks.*

"*Jim thinks I should tell Sawyer everything. What if I tell him and he leaves me?*"

"*That's just fear. Do you remember your nightmare? When you called for Sawyer? When you called for me? We didn't save you. The only one that can save you is you. Remember that. You'll open up to Sawyer when you're ready.*"

"*What am I going to do without you? You always have the right words to say.*"

"*I'm sorry, Ian. I wouldn't have left you if the choice were mine. I hope you know that.*"

"*Jim is going to bring you home as soon as they'll let him. We will do something really nice for you. I bet your brother is going to cook for days.*"

The bartender wipes the counter in front of us.

"Last call."

"Jubal, can I come back and see you tomorrow?"

Jubal gives me another beautiful smile and heads toward the back door. He looks at me over his shoulder. "All you need to do is dream a little dream."

I wake up when Jim opens the door to let CJ out. I roll over without opening my eyes. I beg for sleep to take me back to Sylvia's. I don't want to wake up. It's no use. I close my eyes as tight as I can but it's hopeless.

I know Jim has gone outside to do his chores. He's also doing the work of two farmhands. I grab my pillow and scream, loud and hard. I scream until I'm breathless. Tears and saliva soak my pillow.

Jubal's words play in my head. "The only one that can save you is you."

I wipe my face on my shirt, kick off the covers and get dressed. I'm not going to shatter into a million pieces. I have to better myself every day. I promised Jim. I also promised to do chores. I put on a Freedom Farms cap and head downstairs.

Jim is sitting at the table. His shoulders sag.

"Why aren't you doing your chores?" I ask quietly.

"I was." Jim clears his throat. "Come here. I want to show you something."

Jim leads the way to a shop behind the barn. The sun shines through the open doors onto a large wooden sign. The engraved sign has an oilcan in one corner and a wrench in the other with *JV's Garage* in the center.

"Jim. It's beautiful. You made this? It's exactly how Jubal said he pictured it!"

"With Sawyer's help. It was our gift to you guys." Jim takes his handkerchief from his pocket and blows his nose loudly.

"I'm sorry. I know you loved him. And I know he loved you. We talked about you all the time."

I don't share my dream with him. It's mine. I will keep it to myself.

Chapter Twenty-Two

"Let me know when you're ready for dessert. I made cream cheese brownies. Steve loves them." Patty gives her husband a wink.

"Mom, that was delicious. Thank you." Sawyer kisses his mom on the cheek.

"It really was a great meal. I can't wait for brownies. I should take CJ for a walk before dessert." I push in my seat, wishing I hadn't had seconds.

Sawyer holds my hand. "I'm so proud of you. You're working your butt off at the farm and getting your studying in."

"I promised Jim I would. The blisters on my hands are gross. The gloves at the farm are too big for me, so I end up taking them off. Not my brightest idea." I hold up my free hand to show Sawyer.

"Why didn't you tell Jim? He'll get you gloves that fit." He loosens his grip on my hand. "Am I hurting you?"

I smile at his kindness. "No. They don't hurt too much. I don't want to complain. He's done so much for me."

"Asking for gloves that fit isn't complaining. I'll take you to the store tomorrow and we'll get you a pair."

"You are so sweet. I've got to remember to thank your parents for raising such a sweet guy." I stop walking and hug him.

We walk around letting CJ sniff every plant, bush, and rock we pass. I listen to Sawyer's adventures of flying to Montana and Idaho trying to get the stores up and running. He's learning a lot. "Your dad is so proud of you. I can tell by the way he lights up when he talks about work."

"He's great."

"They both are. I like being around them. Your mom is so good at mom stuff."

"*Mom stuff?* I'll have to remember to tell her that," he says, and smiles.

"You know, like baking and sewing." I pinch his arm. "Don't tease me!"

"Ouch! I'm sorry! Jeez."

We head back inside for dessert and a game of UNO. I can see why these brownies are Steve's favorite. I want to eat four more. But I do not ask for seconds.

I tell them all good night and thank them for a fun evening. Patty hands me a plate of brownies to take home for Jim. Sawyer walks me to my car.

"I was thinking about taking the boat out this weekend. Do you want to go?" He closes my door and leans his arms on my window.

"That sounds great. I wish we could get Jim to go with us." Jim does not like water. He will fish from the beach or wade in a river. But he will not get on a boat.

"Yeah, good luck with that." He pats CJ's head and kisses me one more time. "Call me when you get home. I want to know you're safe."

Sawyer is so good to me. He's very patient. I love that he's not smothering me and he doesn't try to fix me. Nothing can fix me. I have to keep my promise to Jim and better myself every day.

"There they are, Fancy. I told you they'd be back." Jim is reading a newspaper with Fancy at his feet.

"Here are some brownies from Patty. They are amazing." I hand Jim the plate and know by the way his eyes light up that he's had them before.

"Honey, get me some milk, will ya?" He looks adoringly at the plate of chocolaty squares.

I pour two glasses and join Jim back in the living

room. "Here you go … and I'll take one of these."

"Hey! You didn't say I had to share!" He pouts. "Did you have a good time?"

"I did. His parents are cool. It feels good to laugh again. Steve tells the worst jokes!"

"I know. But he's so animated when he tells them." Jim sips his milk in between bites of brownie.

The fire is toasty. I set my glass of milk on the coffee table and run upstairs to change into my pajamas. I get comfortable wrapped up on the couch with CJ on my lap. Jim goes back to reading his paper.

"We have some work left to do on the garage, you know?" Jim says over his newspaper.

"What?" I'm confused. "Are you selling it?"

"No. The garage is yours. Not like I'm giving it to you. The paperwork has your name on it, right below Jubal's."

I sit up and turn to him in disbelief. "He put *my* name on the papers?" Tears flood my eyes instantly.

"I didn't want to tell you before. I wanted to give you time to adjust to being here. It's been hard on both of us, but I don't think I could've made it this last month without you." Jim's voice breaks.

Jubal told me it was our place. I thought he just meant I'd be with him, but he really did mean it when he renamed the garage. My heart is so full of love and sadness I lie back on my pillow and cover my face with my arms.

"We'll go first thing in the morning. Ricky and Marcus can handle things around here." Jim goes back to reading his paper.

I nod my head. I can't wait to fall asleep and see Jubal again. Sometimes he's in my dreams and sometimes I fight off the rats. I hope I can tell him how much I appreciate his gift. I'll promise him I will do everything I can to make him proud. I'll tell him he'll always be with me.

After I collect myself, I give Jim a hug. "Thank you."

I let the dogs out and rinse out our milk glasses before heading upstairs to shower. I can't help but cry. I've waited for a long time to work with Jubal in the garage. I can't imagine opening it without him. He'd said the house behind the garage was a disaster, but beautiful. I hope he will let me stay here until I can fix it up. I let the hot water wash my thoughts down the drain.

"Good morning." Jim kisses the top of my head. "Did you get any sleep last night?"

"A little. No dreams." I'm disappointed.

"Here." Jim hands me a breakfast burrito. "That's a good thing, ain't it?"

"I guess. I'm scared. I don't know how to walk in there without him."

"With one foot in front of the other. And this." Jim holds up the urn containing Jubal's ashes.

I carried that urn around the house for two days after Jim brought it home. I felt guilty for leaving *him* sitting somewhere alone. I know he's not in there, not really, but I couldn't put it down. It wasn't until I saw my reflection that I realized how silly I was being. Jim never said a word. He let me deal with it the only way I knew how. When I finally put the urn on the hearth and left it there, Jim simply said *thank you.*

Jim pulls up to the garage. "Did Jubal show you the house?"

"No. It was always dark when we came through town. He said it was a great place but it needed a lot of work."

We walk around the side of the garage to the house. The bushes have been cleaned up. The yard that was hidden is now visible. There is a cute little fence with a brick sidewalk leading up to the door. The house is quite plain. There is one window looking over the yard and an awning covering the simple door.

"You should know that lake houses aren't built with much attention to the back side." Jim laughs.

"The back is uglier than this?"

"This *is* the back!" Jim lets out a loud belly laugh.

"I didn't mean ugly. It's just, it's so plain." I feel the warmth in my cheeks.

Jim opens the screen and unlocks the door. He waves me inside ahead of him. "After you."

The door leads into the kitchen. "Jim! This is beautiful!" The entire kitchen looks brand new. I can smell the fresh paint. "When did you do this?" I set the urn on the counter.

"I've been working on it for a while now. I took the money Jubal gave me and put it back into this place. It's furnished, but if you don't like anything we can deal with that later." Jim waves his hand towards the doorway. "Go on. Check out the rest of the place."

I walk into a large room with enormous windows that look out to the lake. The view takes my breath away. I walk to the windows and stare out to the water. There's a beautiful deck that runs the length of the house. Beyond the deck are stairs that lead to a dock.

"Jim! It's gorgeous! How do I get out there?" I turn and see Jim smiling from ear to ear.

"The sliding glass door." He reaches in front of me and flips the lock before sliding the door open.

We step outside and the view is the most beautiful thing I've ever seen. The sun is dancing on the water. I can see why Jubal thought of this place as his sanctuary. There are two Adirondack chairs on either side of a wooden table.

Back inside I notice the furniture. The couch looks comfortable, but it's the familiar recliner that catches my attention. Jubal's recliner. "How did you get that?"

"I brought it over when I was able to collect his belongings. If it's too difficult, I can remove it." Jim suddenly looks sad.

"No. It's fine. I'm going to love snuggling in it and watching the sunset. It's perfect."

"I hope you feel the same way about the Blazer, because it's parked in the garage."

"Seriously? I was wondering about that. I get to *keep* it?"

Jim nods. There's a small bedroom with a twin bed and a dresser. The bathroom is green. Green linoleum. Green sink. Green tub.

"I think somebody loves the color green." I wrinkle my nose.

"I didn't have time to remodel the bathrooms. It's solid, though. Everything works. No leaks and good water pressure." He leads us upstairs to check out the master bedroom.

The walls are a soft yellow. A large bed is centered on the wall facing one large window looking over the lake. There's a nook with built-in shelving on either side of the window.

"I expect you to fill these shelves with books. You can travel the world without leaving your bedroom." Jim smiles. "Take a look at your bathroom. It's not green."

Jim is right. It's not green. The bathroom is pink. I love it. It's girly. The bathtub is enormous. I step inside.

"Jim, we can both fit in this thing!"

"Well, what do you think? Can you live in a place like this?"

"You did a fantastic job. The furniture you picked is really great." I walk back into the bedroom. "This bed set is very pretty, Jim." I trace the yellow flowers with my fingers.

Jim walks to the window and sits on the cushion. "I'm sorry Jubal isn't here."

"I'm sad too." I sit next to him, hooking my arm in his. "I'm glad you're here, though."

"You're a sweet girl, Ian. Never change."

"Jim?"

"Yeah?"

"Jubal *is* here. He'll always be with us."

"Sweet and smart. Sawyer's a lucky guy."

Jim locks the door and we open the garage. Seeing the Blazer is too much for both of us.

"How 'bout we go fishing?" I look up at Jim.

"I like the way you think."

Chapter Twenty-Three

"Ian. Sawyer's here," Jim calls up to me.

"I'm almost ready."

I finish brushing my teeth and meet Sawyer in the kitchen. CJ is wagging her tail wildly. She knows it's fishing day. Jim took me to a beautiful river to fish a few weeks ago, but he still will not join us on the boat.

"Are you sure you won't change your mind?" I ask with hands folded in prayer.

"I like my feet on solid ground." Jim shakes his head in protest.

Sawyer opens my door for me. I never tire of this. I kiss him on the mouth before hopping into his pickup. CJ is comfy in the back with her head over the side of the bed, tongue out and tail wagging. The smile on my face is enormous.

"I am so happy today."

"I love the smile on your face, that's for sure. And, I'm sorry I had to postpone our day on the lake. The store in Idaho is struggling to get going. The orders for inventory have been a complete mess twice. Anyway, I'm sorry."

"Don't worry about it. I love that my boyfriend is so smart he has to fly off and fix things!" I flex my muscles and give him a superhero smile.

"Ha ha. That's me, Super Sawyer."

"I can't believe I'm almost eighteen. I think I'm most excited about the test! I want my diploma and I want to start classes at the community college in the fall."

I am excited to test, but really, I'm most excited to be free.

We park at the yacht club and grab our cooler and CJ before making our way to the boat. Sawyer waves to everyone. I just stare at the wooden slats beneath my feet.

I wonder if I will someday walk by people and offer a friendly smile or a simple handshake. I doubt it. I do manage to say hello to Ms. June.

"I think you should look into a public speaking class."

I want to laugh, but he is looking at me with a serious face. "*Public speaking*?"

"Yep. I took one and I learned a lot. The class gives you tools on how to deal with people in different situations. I think it might help you relax a little bit." Sawyer squeezes my hand and flashes his beautiful smile.

I step onto the boat and let CJ wander. Sawyer fires up the boat and guides us out onto the open water. The sun is out but barely. We find a spot and drop anchor. The hours pass, and our catch is quite impressive. The sun is directly over us. I put a towel on the bench and then lie back, watching Sawyer reel in a large fish. I could live a thousand years and never tire of this view.

"I'm hungry."

"I'll go down and fix our sandwiches. I brought some macaroni salad too."

"Girl! You know how to treat me right." Sawyer grabs me and leads me down into the cabin.

Sawyer washes his hands and flings water on my face. I hold out the butter knife in a threatening manner, and he holds his hands up in surrender. I place the knife on the counter and wrap my arms around his neck, pulling his face down to mine and kissing him. That same butterfly feeling I had in my tummy the first time on the boat is happening again. I remember what happened the last time I threw myself on him and pull away.

"I'm sorry. I don't know what it is about this boat, but it brings out the slutty-girl in me." I try to force the blush from my cheeks.

"I don't think you're slutty." Sawyer kisses me softly on the mouth.

We eat our lunch. Sawyer tells me more about his struggles with the new store. I tell him about my plans for the garage. I clean up our mess while Sawyer goes out to put away the poles.

"All clean down there."

"Oh, really? It looks like you have a little something on your face. Right…" He points at my face while stepping slowly towards me.

"Where?" I'm wiping my face with the back of my hand. "Did I get it?"

"Almost. Here, lemme help!" Sawyer wraps me up, lifting me into his arms, and jumps overboard.

CJ is barking, running back and forth, not knowing what to do. She jumps overboard, joining us in the water. I didn't know how hard it was to laugh while trying to float and keep a once-runt-turned-mammoth-sized retriever from pulling me underwater. Until now.

"Here, take my hand." Sawyer reaches out to me after getting himself and CJ onboard.

I take his hand, but then pull with all of my might and laugh as he falls clumsily back into the water. I'm clinging to the transom, laughing hysterically. Sawyer bursts up out of the water choking and laughing.

"Oh… you are in for it now!" He grabs me, trying to loosen my grip. I squeal.

"No! Let me go!"

I climb up first and step far away so Sawyer cannot toss me back into the lake. I wring the water from my hair and shirt. I have a bathing suit on but wasn't given the option of taking off my clothes before being thrown overboard.

Sawyer watches me take my wet clingy clothes

off. I blush.

"What are you staring at?"

"The most beautiful girl I've ever seen."

Suddenly, I'm embarrassed to be standing there in my bathing suit. Sawyer steps closer to me, pulls his shirt off and steps in so we are touching, then leans down and kisses me. It's a long kiss. Our hands are roaming over each other's wet skin. Sawyer moves us to the cushions, guiding me onto his lap without interrupting the kiss. My heart is beating so hard I'm worried he can feel it.

He moves my hair to one side, kissing my neck. I might explode. His hands wrap around me, pulling me closer to his body. I let my tongue play with his and am pleased that his grip on me tightens even more. He makes a trail of kisses from my lips to my neck and down towards my breast, then stops.

I open my eyes to see him fixed on the now-healed scar on my chest. He has a sad look on his face. I take his hand in mine and scoot off his lap to sit next to him. I have no words, so I just lean my head on his shoulder and sit in silence.

Sawyer wraps his arm around me, kissing the top of my head. "I think we should call it a day."

"Okay." Again I'm unable to tell him what I've been through. The bad things I've done will make him look at me differently. I know it.

The drive to Jim's is quiet. I stare out the window, replaying our make-out session in my head: His soft lips. The way his hands know my body so well. I look over at him and he looks at me with a half-hearted smile.

"I'll be back later. I have some errands to take care of for my mom." Sawyer kisses me and closes my door.

"Come on, CJ."

I watch him drive away and hope he returns.

~~~~~~~

"How was fishing?" Jim joins me on the porch step.

"I'm a freak. Do you know that? I'm a messed up, wrecked person. We were having a great day and I ruined it."

"Calm down. What do you mean you ruined it?"

I tell Jim about the afternoon, taming down the hotter points. I hate that I have a permanent reminder of the scariest night of my life. I try to pretend it doesn't look like a bite mark, but I know it. Sawyer knows it.

"I think you're doing yourself an injustice by keeping your experiences from Sawyer. He loves you. He's not worried about your past."

"I don't even know where to start. The whole thing is just messed up!"

Jim pets CJ and listens to me ramble on with the million excuses I have for not telling Sawyer. He has a rebuttal for each one.

"Well, we don't have to keep beating a dead horse. Go on in and wash that lake water off of you and CJ."

"Okay, Jim. Dinner smells delicious. Did you make your rolls? You know I love your rolls more than life itself, don't you?"

"I've learned to keep a steady ration of dinner rolls around here since you moved in."

I bathe CJ and Fancy before climbing into a hot shower. I keep seeing the sad look on Sawyer's face. I should've kept my shirt on. "Yeah, that's the solution, stupid."

Jim asks me to set the table. "Set it for seven."

"Seven?" I stuff pieces of a warm roll in my

mouth.

"Yes, ma'am. I invited Steve and Patty to dinner when I saw them in town this morning."

"Oh, cool. I hope Steve has his jokes ready." I smile and toss another piece of dinner roll in my mouth.

"I'm glad I made extra. You eat like a sumo wrestler. I honestly don't know where you put it."

After I set the table, I run upstairs to get ready. I've been practicing braiding my hair the way Patty taught me. It's not as good as when she fixes it, but I'm getting better. I apply a little mascara and lip-gloss but wipe my lips after looking in the mirror. The makeup only accents the features of my mother.

I visit with Ricky and Marcus while Jim finishes up dinner. Marcus tells me his niece is having her second baby any day now. Ricky doesn't say much, as usual. He just smiles and enjoys everyone's stories.

I'm telling the guys about the fish Sawyer caught when there's a knock at the door. "I'll get it!" I walk to the living room, taking a quick glimpse in the mirror by the front door.

"Oh, Ian! You're getting so much better with the braiding." Patty circles me, checking my work.

"Thank you. I'm so glad you two are joining us. I had such a good day on the lake. Your boat is amazing." I blush a little bit at the memory of Sawyer's bare chest.

We all sit down at the dining table. There is rarely a moment of silence. One story is followed by another. Steve sneaks a joke in between stories of expecting family members and fishing. I have a permanent smile on my face, as I take it all in. These people are so important to me. I can't picture my life without them. I know Jubal wanted this life for me. He wanted me to be surrounded by people who are kind and loving.

"So, Ian. I hear you are turning eighteen in a few days." Marcus smiles. "If only I could be turning eighteen again. The things I'd do differently."

"She's got big plans. Don't you, Ian?" Jim raises his glass to me.

"I do. I will be testing for my diploma. Once I have that, I'll work at the garage until I can afford to start classes at MVCC."

"That's a great plan." Ricky says in his quiet voice. "You're going to do fine."

"I know I've had a lot of people asking about the garage. Lots of compliments on the work you're doing around there. It looks so bright and clean. I bet you'll have plenty of business." Patty pats my hand and smiles proudly.

I'm overwhelmed with the center of attention being on me. "Jim, did you make cobbler?" This attempt backfires, as they all begin to talk about my appetite.

"Are you sure you're not eating for two?" Marcus laughs.

The room goes instantly silent. All eyes are bouncing off me and Sawyer, like they are all watching a tennis match.

"No! Oh, gosh! No, I'm not pregnant!"

"She's always eaten like a horse," Jim chimes in.

"I'll be in the kitchen dishing up dessert and dying of embarrassment." I clumsily stumble out of the dining room.

Chapter Twenty-Four

"You'll be fine." Sawyer takes my hand to calm me. "You've been studying for months. You're one of the smartest people I know."

"You promise you'll be back in time to take me? I'm so nervous."

"I promise." Sawyer kisses me on the top of my messy hair.

I stand in the driveway, waving goodbye in my pajamas and bedhead. Sawyer has another trip to meet with potential store-owners. Steve's idea to use local farmer's for the majority of the hay and corn is getting more and more popular. It builds communities in so many ways. I never get tired of listening to them talk about it.

There's only three days until my appointment to test. I go upstairs to change and find Jim in the barn with Lulu.

"She looks beautiful. Sawyer says hello. He came by to say goodbye. He's so sweet. I've been kind of grouchy with all the stress and studying."

"Really? I hadn't noticed." Jim gives me a crooked grin.

"I'm sorry! I just want this so much."

Jim asks what I want for my birthday-slash-graduation party.

"The usual spread, of course."

"I pretty much had the menu sorted out. I mean, what do you want for your gift?"

"I don't want anything. You've already given me so much, Jim." I've never expected a gift for accomplishing anything. The question alone makes me smile.

"That's helpful. I guess I'll just have to get creative."

Jim insists that I do not study any more. "You're just going to overload your brain. I know you'll be fine. I think what we need to do is take the quads out for a nice long trek."

"That sounds amazing. I need to take care of the pigs first, then I'll help you with lunch."

"Ah, yes. Lunch." Jim winks at me. "Like we'd forget food."

Jim loads the quads onto the trailer and he drives us into the mountains. We follow a trail high up into the hills. Jim points out a bald eagle and a mountain lion off in the distance. The breeze feels wonderful. The tall pines dance above us.

Jim parks at a clearing. We climb up on some rocks and prepare a little picnic. I can tell he is trying to tell me something, but seems unable to find the words.

"What?"

"It really freaks me out when you do that." Jim hands me a sandwich.

"Spill it."

"Eat your food and let me collect my thoughts, honey."

I easily change my focus from a conversation to food. I lean back on the rock behind me, letting the sun hit my face. I'm about to doze off when Jim finally decides to speak.

"You know you mean the world to me, right? So, when I talk to you about things I need you to keep that in mind."

"You're freaking me out, now. Just talk to me."

"You've been studying very hard. You've been working very hard. What I need to know is if what you're working so hard for is what you want."

"The garage was Jubal's dream. He gave me a

piece of that dream."

"But is it *your* dream?" Jim wipes his face with his handkerchief.

"I never had a dream. My only plan was to get out of my parents' house. I wanted to escape the nightmare that was my life. Jubal took me in and shared his passion of working on cars with me. It became my plan to do that with him."

"Right, honey. But is it your passion? I don't want you to burn yourself out on all this working and studying only to realize it's not what you want. The garage is yours. The house is yours. You can do whatever you want."

I never thought about what I wanted for my future. I only thought of a future once Jubal made me happy to be alive. I took in everything he taught me. It just seemed natural that I'd continue with our plan. But, is it really my passion?

"I don't know."

"I figured as much. And that's okay. You don't have to know. I want you to be aware that you have options."

"It's weird but I feel less stressed knowing that. Thank you. And Jim? You don't have to be afraid to talk to me—about anything. I talk to you about everything!"

We ride for a while longer before heading back down to the truck. Riding is exhausting so we both want to shower and go right to bed. I curl up with CJ and fall asleep with the hopes of seeing Jubal in my dreams.

I wake and rush downstairs. I'm disappointed that I didn't dream, but I'm so energized. I turn eighteen tomorrow. Jim is already doing his chores. I make coffee and rush out to find him.

"Jim! Jim!" I find him with the chickens. "Good

morning! I am so excited for tomorrow … you might have to knock me out at bedtime! I am finally going to test for my diploma."

"Good morning. Are you sure you don't want to have your party until after you get your score? We can have a party tomorrow and a party when you get your diploma."

"No. I want to wait. The proctor at the testing center said it'd take seven business days. I can wait that long. And, Jim? I thought about what you told me. You got me thinking about what makes me happy and what I'm passionate about."

"What did you come up with?"

"I'm passionate about life. I love being with you here at the farm. I love being in the garage working on greasy engines. I am so happy when I think about opening the garage. I'm happy because it's my passion. Sure, it was Jubal's dream but it's my dream now, too. Thank you for asking me to look inside and see what I want for my future."

"You're a special girl, Ian. I hope you know that."

"Thank you, Jim. I can't believe tomorrow morning will change me forever. I'll never have to look over my shoulder in fear of being hauled back to that hellhole. I'll never have to fear them again."

"You haven't had to worry about that since the morning you got on the back of Jubal's bike. He never would've let you go back. And I wouldn't have either. But, you're right. You'll be your own person tomorrow."

I wave and get busy on my chores. I won't miss the pigpen but I will miss the morning routine that has become second nature to me. It's exciting to think I'll be in my own place soon. I'll be waking up to see the gorgeous view of the lake. I wonder if I'll be able to point out Steve's boat from my deck.

I finish lunch with Jim and the guys. "I think I'm going to go look over the college paperwork."

"Sounds good, Ian."

I flip through the brochure. The lady at the counseling office told me I can decide on what I want to get a degree in but I'll need prerequisites for all of them, which means I will start with math, English and science courses.

A knock on my door wakes me. "Come in."

Sawyer walks through my door. "This doesn't look like filling out paperwork."

"Sawyer! What time is it?" Did I sleep through the night? Did I miss my appointment? Am I eighteen?"

"It's almost time for dinner. Relax. You didn't miss anything." Sawyer laughs at me.

"That stuff is so boring." I wipe the slobber from my chin.

"It really is. Are you ready for tomorrow?"

"I am." My bedhead says otherwise.

I find Jim in the kitchen with Ricky and Marcus. Sawyer wishes me luck on my test. The rest are in agreement that I'm going to ace the test.

"I hope you're all right! Tomorrow is a huge day for me. I am so lucky to have you guys here with me."

Sawyer tells me to get a good night's sleep before heading home. "I'll pick you up at eight. Bye, guys."

I offer to clean up the kitchen but Ricky tells me he and Marcus will take care of it. Marcus pretends to complain, but doesn't fool anyone.

I lay out my clothes for the morning and crawl into bed. My mind is all over the place. I force my thoughts to clear until I am only focusing on my breathing.

~~~~~~~~

"Happy birthday." Sawyer whispers. "Happy birthday."

"I'm eighteen?" I mumble.

"You are. And you have a big day ahead of you. Good morning! Happy birthday!" He hugs me and kisses the top of my head.

Sawyer drives me to the testing center. I have my ID and proper forms in hand. He opens the door for me and walks me to the door.

"You can do this. Just relax and try not to throw up on the proctor. They don't like it."

Sawyer always knows how to make me laugh. My shoulders relax instantly.

"You'll be here waiting for me?"

"I'll be back here in three hours. Good luck, Ian." Sawyer kisses me before heading back to the parking lot.

I find Room 1216 and introduce myself to a very tall woman who has extremely large gums. She takes my information and hands me the test.

"You have four hours to complete the test. Any answers left incomplete will be counted as incorrect. You may have one bathroom break, but may not use any notes or make any phone calls until the test is complete. Do you have any questions?" Gladys is all business.

"No, Ma'am. Thank you."

"Your time starts now," Gladys announces, once I've settled into my seat with the paper test and a No. 2 pencil.

Sawyer is sitting on the bench outside. He jumps up to greet me.

"How'd you do? I bet you killed it!"

"I don't know. It's all a blur."

"It's time to celebrate! How does a banana split sound? My mom makes the best in the world."

"That sounds great!"

I'm surprised to see Jim and the guys when I walk in. They all make a big fuss about my birthday. Patty has baked a cake, with "*Happy Birthday, Ian*" written in purple cursive letters.

I smile as tears of happiness spill onto my cheeks. I've never had so many happy people singing 'Happy Birthday' to me. I am finally free.

Chapter Twenty-Five

"Jim! You open it! I can't!" I hand Jim the large manila envelope.

"Okay." Jim takes the envelope, opening it slowly. "Are you sure you want to know the results?"

"Jim!" I'm dancing with anticipation.

"Dear Miss Ross…"

"No!" I hold up my hand. "Okay, tell me."

"The California State Board of Education is pleased to inform you that you've *successfully achieved your high school diploma!*" Jim reads with excitement.

"I did it?"

"You did it!" Jim hugs me. "I'm so proud of you! Looks like that party Friday night is *on!*"

"I've gotta call Sawyer!" I clumsily dial the number.

The guys come in and congratulate me. "I knew you'd do great!" Marcus pats my shoulder.

Jim leaves the kitchen while Marcus and Ricky tell me how proud of me they are. When Jim returns, he hands me a tiny wrapped box.

"I can't wait until your party to give you this. I know you said you didn't want anything but that's not my style. I hope you like it."

I sit at the table and slowly unwrap the paper. Beneath the paper is a dark blue box. I open it to see a gold necklace with my name in cursive writing. *Vivian.*

"Jim. It's beautiful. I love it." I take the necklace from its box and hold it out to show the guys. "Help me put it on, please."

I hold my hair out of the way and after the necklace is clasped I keep holding it and looking down at my shiny gold name.

Jim isn't the only one with gifts. Marcus gives me

a nice leather messenger bag for school and Ricky has a gift certificate for Mervyn's.

"I figure you can buy yourself some new clothes for school…" Ricky says in his small voice.

"Thank you, guys." I wipe my tear-soaked cheeks. "This is so special."

Sawyer comes in with his parents, who are holding even more gifts. Sawyer rushes to me and pulls me in for a big hug.

"I am so proud of you. We all are." Sawyer kisses my cheek.

"Here." Patty hugs me and gives me her gift. "This is from Steve and me. It's nothing fancy."

I open a card and pull out a gift certificate from *Solomon and Son Home Security Systems*.

"We figure we'll all sleep a little better knowing you have some added protection. These guys are the best in the area. You'll be set up with a great system!" Steve expounds.

"That's a great idea," Jim says, taking the business card to further examine.

Sawyer pulls me to the side. "I want to give you my gift later."

"Okay."

"You know, I've gotta say … I'm really starting to love our gatherings. You guys are spoiling me."

Patty brings up the party plans. "I'm bringing the cake and decorations."

"We don't need to have a party. This is perfect." I wave my hand like the idea is an annoying fly.

"Oh, don't be silly. A dinner or two does not a party make."

"I guess you can't argue with that." Steve gives me a wink.

I show everyone the gifts I've received and still am unable to leave the necklace alone.

The food is delicious as usual. Ricky heads out first, followed shortly after by Steve and Patty. Marcus is in a deep conversation with Jim about cattle prices. Sawyer nods in the direction of my room. I follow him upstairs.

"I've been waiting to get you alone." Sawyer pulls me in for a long kiss.

"Is this my present? Because if it is, I'd like more, please."

We crawl onto my bed and lie there talking. "No. This isn't your gift. Kissing you is a gift to *me*. I knew you'd do great on the test."

"I was so excited when Jim read the letter. And he was just as excited, if not more."

Jim comes up after a while and tells us good night. I ask Sawyer if he'll stay a little while longer.

"I have to fly out Saturday. The new store in Oregon is getting close to their final stages before opening. I'm going to really need patience with this one."

"You know how to handle these people. I've seen you work your charm."

"I want to make your party a memorable night. That is why you can't have your gift until then."

~~~~~~~~~

I close my eyes for a second and before I know, Sawyer is nudging me awake. "I fell asleep. I guess when I'm in bed with you … my body won't let me leave."

"I have a confession. You fell asleep before I did."

"I did? " Sawyer begins tickling me. "You let me fall asleep?"

Downstairs is quiet. I'm guessing the guys are all

out doing their chores.

"Are you hungry? I can make you some eggs."

"No, thank you. I should get going. I need to get packed and ready for my flight. Steve and I leave early."

"Okay. I'll see you later then."

"You better get to your chores, young lady." Sawyer kisses me and quickly steps towards the front door.

"You better go!" I swing a hand towel at him.

I find Jim leaning on the gate, watching Lulu prance in the yard. I can tell when he's given her a good brushing. "She is so pretty."

"Good morning." Jim looks over his shoulder. "I had the guys take over your chores. I figure you'll be moving into the lake house soon so they should get back to their old schedule."

"How can I be so excited and scared at the same time?"

"You'll be great. And, I'm always here for you. You know that?"

"I do." I pat his back. "But I can't not do my chores. I'm going to clean the pigpen or collect eggs from the coop." I wave goodbye to Jim and make my way to the chickens. Ricky can handle the pigs.

It seems like only minutes pass before Jim's hollering that it's lunchtime. I've been so busy working I didn't hear my stomach growling.

I walk in the kitchen door and see Sawyer setting the table. "Hi, Sawyer! I'm going to run up and take a shower. I smell awful."

"You sure do. Phew! Blecch!" Sawyer and Jim tease me.

Ricky and Marcus have joined the guys at the table. Marcus is quick to start a conversation as usual.

"Hey, Ian. Are you excited for tonight? We've got a big bonfire ready to go."

"Really? I'm very excited! I love a good bonfire." I grab my heavy plate adorned with a moose head and pinecone trim. "Almost as much as I love fried chicken!"

I seriously consider picking up my plate to lick it clean but decide against it. Ricky and Marcus get back to work. Sawyer helps me collect the plates and silverware. Jim feeds the dogs. There's a knock at the front door. Jim offers to get it, as Sawyer and I are elbows deep in the soapy water.

Moments later, Jim comes into the kitchen. I turn around expecting to see Patty and Steve but instead I'm facing a tall skinny man with a yellow tint to his skin wearing a dark suit that is at least two sizes too large for him.

"Miss Ross?" He sets a banker's box on one of the dining table chairs.

Something clamps my throat closed. "I'm not going back. I don't have to! Jim! Tell him!" I back toward the door.

Sawyer is staring at me and Jim in wide-eyed confusion. He is still holding the scrubbing brush that is now dripping onto the floor.

"Ian. Please sit down. Mr. Danner is not here to take you anywhere."

It takes Jim several minutes to convince me it's safe for me to have a seat across from the suit-wearing stranger. I choose the seat closest to the door in case I need to make a run for it.

"Hi, Vivian. As Jim said, my name is Mr. Danner." He holds out a hand and I hesitate before quickly shaking his bony hand.

"I'm not sure how to start this, so I'll be blunt.

There's been an accident."

"I don't understand." I look to Jim expecting him to clear this up for me. He cannot.

"Your parents were in an accident. They didn't survive."

The room spins like a kaleidoscope. I don't know what the man just said but when he finishes speaking, the room that I was standing in has morphed into tiny specks of color dancing on the walls and ceiling.

Jim is in front of me, moving his lips slowly. "Ian, you need to control your breathing. Listen to my voice. Please sit down and try to relax." I have moved towards the door.

Mr. Danner continues his explanation. "The accident happened six months ago. I am your mother's lawyer—well, I *was* her lawyer. When she made her will she had explicit instructions that I was only to find you once you were of legal age, if anything were to happen."

I feel something squeeze my hand. I turn to see Sawyer looking at me in disbelief. Of course he's in shock. My parents have died for the second time. I can't explain that right now.

"You are their only next of kin. You are the beneficiary of their estate. I need a signature, and then I will be on my way." He keeps talking but I cannot make out his words.

It's weird to see a stranger standing in front of me with tears close to spilling onto his cheeks while discussing my parents' deaths.

"Do you have any questions?" Mr. Danner is sitting next to me, shaking like I might attack him.

"I have two." I look at Sawyer and his face has changed from shock to a mixture of sadness and anger. "Were they drunk?"

"Yes, ma'am."

"Was anyone else hurt?"

"No, ma'am."

I focus on my breathing, forcing the little specks of color into their places. "I don't want anything from them."

Jim doesn't wait to put me in my place. "Ian. You will take what was left to you. You can use the money to help with school."

"Fine. Where do I sign?" I take the pen and wait for Mr. Danner to steady his hand enough to show me the signature line.

I'm about to put the tip of the pen to the paper when I see Sawyer storm out of the kitchen. I jump up to follow him, leaving Jim and Mr. Danner in the kitchen discussing details.

"Sawyer! Please wait." I have to run to his pickup to catch up to him.

"What?" He has tears in his eyes.

"I'm sorry." These two words are the only ones I can manage.

"Sorry? I don't want you to be sorry. My condolences." He continues to his truck.

"What do you want me to say?"

He stops in his tracks and turns on me quickly. "Oh, I don't know. You can tell me about … your dead parents? Yeah, tell me about them. Or maybe … *the fucking bite* on your chest."

His words hit me like a sledgehammer. I'm not ready for his anger. Sobs build in my chest and my bottom lip is quivering.

"You know, I've never once pushed you for anything. I figured you'd tell me when you trusted me. I know nothing about you. I know absolutely nothing about you." Sawyer gets in his truck and drives away, leaving me crying in the driveway.

I step back into the kitchen and pour myself some coffee. Tears are streaming down my cheeks, making wet circles on my shirt. Jim is still having a discussion with Mr. Danner.

"Ian. I think you should sit down and listen to Mr. Danner."

"I'm sorry for your loss." He looks up at me with gray eyes.

"I'm not crying because my parents are gone. They've been dead to me since I left that house. I'm crying because they've managed to screw up my life even now, after they're dead."

Mr. Danner decides to jump right in and begin his speech. "I met your mother a little over a year ago, in AA. I eventually became her sponsor. She came to me and asked me to help her with a will. She wanted to make sure you were taken care of if something were to happen to her."

"I believe you have the wrong person. My mother never went to AA." I can feel the anger surfacing in my cheeks.

"She did. Your mother hired a detective to find you. She told me she could never make amends for her wrongs and struggled everyday with her demons. She would come to meetings with bruises sometimes, until she stopped coming altogether."

"The bruises make sense." I feel no pity for her.

I look at the two men and I'm shocked they are staring at me with held breath. They seem disappointed when I stand, not fazed by this bombshell.

"I'll leave my card in case you have any questions." He taps his still-shaking hand on top of the box. "This box holds the items your mother wanted you to have. Everything else was sold, including the house. All proceeds were put into a bank account. It will do a lot more than help with your education."

"I'm out of here." I run upstairs to my room and grab a jacket then bolt out of the front door. I don't know where I'm going but if I stand in the same room with that jaundiced lawyer another second, I'll go crazy.

I keep seeing Sawyer's hurt face. I should've told him.

Chapter Twenty-Six

I drive. Music up. Windows down. The road in front of me is beckoning me to continue. I come up on the sign to turn off to go to Cavern Creek. I keep driving forward. The interstate is crowded with vehicles weaving in and out of the lanes, busily making their way to their destinations. My breath catches as the hills open up and the Reno city lights sparkle under the darkening sky.

My knuckles are white from the death grip I have on the wheel. I exit the freeway, drive through two lights then turn left, then three blocks more, then turn right. I shift into park and kill the engine. I stare at the house across the street. The house I swore I'd never come back to.

It looks exactly the same yet totally different. The gray paint that used to peel at the corners is a bright yellow. The screen that once sat crooked on its hinges now sits perfectly straight. The missing shingles have been replaced. Pink curtains have replaced the vinyl shade I remember hanging in my bedroom window.

I imagine the family is inside enjoying dessert and watching television. Surely, not fighting over spilled paint in the garage.

Tears run freely down my face. I'm not crying for my parents. I'm crying for me, for my lost childhood. Because of them I am broken. I lost Jubal. I lost Sawyer. I never understood what Sawyer saw in me to begin with. He would've left me eventually.

"No! Jubal said I'm good. He said I'm *good*!" I hit the steering wheel as the pain inside proves too much for me to handle. "Jubal! Why'd you leave me?"

I fold my arms over the steering wheel and rest my head. I sit sobbing, with tears and snot running down my face. I open the glove box for tissues and pull out a

Polaroid from the first barbecue at Jim's. They didn't know I took the picture. The two brothers were drinking a beer and reminiscing about a fishing trip when they were young boys. Jubal caught a fish and Jim was trying to get it off the hook when he lost his footing and fell into the river. Their smiles are perfect. I find a tissue and dry my face and look at the picture again.

A knock on the window makes me jump in my seat. I wipe my face on a dry corner of the McDonald's napkin and turn to see Ms. Watson from next door.

"Honey, are you okay?" She jumps back like she'd just seen a ghost.

I roll my window down halfway. "I'm fine, Ms. Watson. I'm leaving."

"Oh, my word. I thought they killed you." Her hands are half covering her face.

"What?"

"You just disappeared one day. I thought they killed you."

"They did." I start the car and drive off with a screech of the tires.

I make my way through the city streets until I pull in front of Sylvia's. I stare at my swollen bloodshot eyes in the rearview mirror and debate whether I should go inside. I can't. I smile as I remember the first night I stood in front of this place. Jubal was so strong. He laughed once, and I loved him. I'm thankful he took me out of the sad world I knew and made it happy.

I drive to the turn-off sign for Cavern Creek. I don't want to see Mikus' house. I don't want to see where Jubal fought for a friend who couldn't have possibly loved him more than I did, and do. I'm afraid if I see that place again I'll shatter into a million pieces.

"Jubal. If you can hear me, I remember everything

you ever taught me. I'm going to make you proud. I promise to be the person you saw in me. I miss you. Thank you for taking me to meet your brother. I can see why you looked up to him. He's taken such good care of me. If I didn't have Jim, I don't know what would've happened to me. I love you, Jubal."

I make the drive into Mission Valley. I pull up to Jim's and find him waiting in the living room.

"I was wonderin' when you'd be back." Jim rubs his eyes and looks at his watch.

I walk into his arms and cry. He holds me and rubs my back as I sob. "I'm… sorry. Sorry I worried you."

"Shhhh. It's okay." Jim keeps an arm around my shoulder and walks me into the kitchen. "Have a seat. I'll fix you some chocolate milk. And get you some toilet tissue."

I laugh involuntarily.

Jim returns from the bathroom and hands me a roll of tissue paper. I blow my nose several times. I'm unable to stop crying.

"I went to Reno." I force my voice to be steady. "I don't know why, but I had to go. I had to see for myself, maybe. I don't know." I sip the chocolate milk Jim gave me.

"I had a feeling. I thought either Reno or Cavern." Jim rubs his eyes again.

"I couldn't go to the house. It's such an ugly place. Such ugly memories. I talked to him—to Jubal. I talked to him most of the way home. Silly, huh?"

"Not at all. I talk to him all the time. Oh, hey—even though your party was canceled, Patty brought the cake. Would you like a piece?"

"No. I'm exhausted. And so are you. I'll have

cake for breakfast."

"I never thought I'd hear you turn down food. Especially cake. But, I'm glad you did. I am dog tired." He kisses the top of my head. "Goodnight, Honey."

I wake to voices down in the kitchen. I try to sit up but my brain is playing tennis inside my head. I try to rub my eyes but they are too raw from all of the crying. I hold my head in my hands and force myself out of bed. I pull on my robe and look in the mirror. I resemble a Japanese sumo wrestler. My face is swollen and my eyes are barely-open slits.

I tiptoe across the hall into the bathroom to wash my face. The cold cloth feels wonderful on my skin. The mirror reveals no difference in my appearance. I open the door and slowly step toward the stairs. The voices grow louder with each step.

"That's too bad. The poor girl," Patty says before sipping her coffee.

"She's not a poor girl, Patty. She's stronger than anyone I've ever known."

"That's not what I mean. Of course, she's strong. She's had to be strong. But even the strongest people can be broken." Patty lifts her head and looks into my eyes.

"Morning. I'm sorry I ruined the party."

"You have nothing to be sorry for. Come here and give me a hug. I was so worried about you."

Jim dishes a big slice of cake and puts it in a bowl of milk. "Here you go. You said you wanted cake for breakfast."

"Thank you, Jim."

"What in the world?" Patty looks at my bowl of now milk-soaked cake.

"This is the only way to eat cake. You should try it." I take a big bite of delicious cake.

"You heard the lady, Jim. I'll take a piece of cake for breakfast too." She looks at me with her kind smile.

Jim hands her a bowl and heads outside. "I'd better get to work."

We sit there eating our cake and drinking coffee, neither one wanting to be the first to talk.

"You're right. This is amazing. I'll never eat a piece of cake the old way again."

"I think Sawyer hates me." I don't look at her when I speak for fear of returning sobs.

"Oh, Honey. He doesn't hate you. I'm sure he's just hurt and confused. He didn't want to talk about it this morning. But, he'll come around."

"I couldn't tell him. I know he didn't think I was perfect but I didn't think he could overlook what I've been through and the things I've done." I get up to refill our coffee.

"Sawyer told me about your parents. I'm very sorry."

"Don't be. Seriously. They were dead to me a long time ago."

"You'll be able to deal with that in time."

"I'm kinda glad Sawyer is gone. I don't want him to see me like this. I look like a zombie."

"He loves you no matter what, Ian."

"I don't know that he's going to forgive me for this."

"Can I ask you why you lied about your parents being dead? And why you couldn't tell Sawyer?"

I put our bowls in the sink and sit back down next to Patty. "I couldn't tell Sawyer. What would I have said? Oh, by the way, my father is the devil and my mother is his satanic bride? You guys are the perfect family. He wouldn't understand. You wouldn't understand."

"We are the perfect family, but not for the reason you think. We are perfect because we love each other. We fight for each other. We are there for each other. That is why we're perfect."

"Sawyer has his mother and father who have loved him his entire life."

"Steve isn't Sawyer's father."

My jaw drops open. "*What*?"

"I met Steve after I left his father. I had two-hundred dollars and a bloody lip when I met him." Patty puts her tongue in her lip to demonstrate how it looked.

"What happened?"

"I made the mistake of marrying my father. Not literally, of course, but an abusive man just like him. He was pure hatred. If he had a bad day at work, he'd cheer himself up by beating me down."

Seeing Patty in this light makes my stomach hurt. How could anyone hurt this wonderful woman? "What made you finally leave?"

"I left him when he turned his anger towards Sawyer. He was called into his boss's office and written up. That happened the same day Sawyer lost his first tooth. Sawyer was so excited he couldn't wait to tell his dad. George stormed in that night and lit right into me. Little Sawyer was tugging at his shirt until George turned from me and slapped him across the face."

"Holy shit!"

"Yeah, holy shit. I grabbed the lamp from the side table and knocked him out. Then I took the grocery money and packed our clothes. I was on a bus to my aunt's house when we stopped in Mission Valley for a switch of drivers. Steve was in the diner."

"No way! Does Sawyer remember this?"

"No. He knows that Steve isn't his biological

father, but there is no question that he is his dad." Patty smiles into her coffee mug.

"He gravitated to Steve from the second he saw him. He actually showed him his missing tooth. He told Steve he worried the tooth fairy might not find him because he wasn't home. Steve made a big deal out of that tooth. He promised the tooth fairy would find him and that he didn't need to worry."

"Patty. My mom didn't leave. I was abused until the day I left. I thought I was bad. I thought I didn't deserve any better. Every day I spent with Jubal was a lesson of who I am and who I'm capable of becoming."

"Steve bought us a room at the motel across from the garage, actually. He wanted to be sure the tooth fairy would be able to do her job. He told me later that he fell in love with us the moment he laid eyes on us."

"You are so lucky. And, you are such a good mom. You've raised an amazing man."

"It's not luck. God is good and has blessed us abundantly." Patty pats my hand. "It's also a lot of hard work. A lot!"

"Did he ever come looking for you? George?"

"Oh, no. He had plenty of girlfriends to keep his mind off of us. He signed the paternity papers without hesitation. Steve proposed the day my divorce was granted. He asked Sawyer if it was okay."

"Paternity papers?"

"It's an affidavit that cancels all rights as a parent. He just gave him up. I was happy but sad. You know? Part of me was happy to have no strings to George, but it hurt to know that he didn't fight for his son."

"It's truly his loss. Sawyer is amazing."

"I agree." She sighs. "I really should be going. I have to lead the quilter's group at the library. There was just no way I could focus on anything until I knew you were safe. Please, don't take off like that again." Patty pats my hand and stands up from the table.

"Thank you for coming to check on me. I was so overwhelmed when Mr. Tanner, or Danner, came in. I thought he was going to take me back to my father."

"I understand. Would you like to come over for a visit tonight? Maybe let me paint your nails again?"

"I'd love to."

Patty makes it to the door when I stop her. "Patty, when will Sawyer and Steve be home?"

"Steve will be home in two days. Sawyer has made arrangements to stay in Oregon for a couple weeks. He just needs some time, Ian."

Chapter Twenty-Seven

"Thanks, guys." Jim closes the door after the installers have taught us how to use the security system.

"I have a phone and a security system. Now all I need are plates, silverware, towels…"

I read off the list I started.

"Well, let's go then. We'll stop by that secondhand shop and get that table you want while we're out." Jim puts the dogs out into the yard while I lock the door.

"Oh, and that lamp for your side table. It'll look great in your living room."

We walk through the store after stocking up on household goods. We finish at the grocery store. I'm glad Jim is with me for this part, because I have no idea what to stock my pantry with.

"Have you heard from Sawyer?" he asks.

"Nope. Patty said he'd be home tomorrow. I haven't talked to him. I think he hates me."

"Don't be silly."

"What's corn starch for?" I change the subject.

"Okay, I get the hint. I'll stop talking about it."

Jim keeps his word and doesn't bring up Sawyer again. He helps me put away the groceries and shows me how to work the new washing machine. We sit on the deck and enjoy the changing colors of the sunset.

"You should fix up that boat on the side of the garage. It's a good one for fishing. I know a guy that can help you." Jim winks at me.

"I love that idea!"

Jim stays long enough to help me line the shelves in the linen closet. He calls Fancy and reminds me to set the alarm after he leaves.

"I'll come by next weekend to help you move the

boat into the garage. Call me after you get your schedule tomorrow."

"Okay. I'll make sure I have that bay cleared out."

I set the alarm and start a fire before climbing into Jubal's recliner. CJ has claimed the other recliner. The radio is playing in the background. I drink my glass of chocolate milk while the sky changes from soft orange and pink to dark blue. My eyes grow heavy.

"I told you this place is amazing. Look at that sky." Jubal sits in the recliner next to me. "You need to work on your fire building skills."

"Shut it! It's not the same being here without you. I hope you don't mind, but I took over your chair."

"I wouldn't have it any other way."

"Jubal..."

~~~~~~~~

I'm jolted awake by the ringing telephone. I stumble into the kitchen to answer it with CJ on my heels. "Jubal?"

"What? No. It's Sawyer. Are you okay?"

"Oh. Hey, Sawyer. I was sleeping. I must've been dreaming."

"I got your number from my mom. She said the place looks great."

"Yeah, your parents came by the other day to bring me a housewarming gift and some casseroles for the freezer. I've been eating at Jim's and coming here just to sleep mostly. I just went grocery shopping today." I play with the phone cord, twisting it around my fingers.

"Ian. I was wondering if I could come by when I get home. I think we need to talk."

"I'd like that."

"I'll see you tomorrow night then. Go back to sleep."

"Good night, Sawyer."

I hang up the phone and look down at CJ. "I'd be more excited if I wasn't so tired."

Morning comes after a restless night's sleep. I forgot to put the towels in the dryer so I have to shower and dry off with my robe. I am supposed to be at the college in forty minutes. I let CJ out to go potty and the alarm goes off. I quickly enter the code to stop the high-pitched beeping and fix my coffee.

"You be a good girl. I'll be home in a little while." I latch the gate and hop into my car.

Two hours later I pull up to the house. I unlock the door and call Jim right away. I read off my schedule. I have business classes in the mornings and automotive in the evenings. "I never realized how much I missed school. The counselor is very nice. I think she's single."

"Oh, good. You should ask her out to a movie." Jim laughs.

"Ha ha. I'm going to work in the garage. I'll call you tomorrow."

I don't tell him about Sawyer calling me or that he's coming over tonight. I don't want to be any more nervous than I am. I go outside to the garage. Seeing the Blazer hurts less each time I see it. I'm not ready to drive it. But I will never get rid of it.

I get the floor sweep out and clean the garage and organize the tools. The box that Mr. Danner left for me sits on the counter by the door. I push the button to close the bay doors and flip off the light. I pick up the box and carry it inside.

I hop in the shower and realize I haven't eaten. Sawyer won't be here for hours, so I have time to clean up and eat. "CJ, I wonder if we'll survive with me in charge." She barks in reply.

I fix myself a turkey sandwich and pour a glass of iced tea. "Come on, CJ. Let's go outside and get some sun."

I change into my bathing suit and lie in the sun. The radio is blaring out some Fleetwood Mac. I tap my foot to the beat, singing along with my best Stevie Nicks impression. CJ brings me her toy and drops it on my chest. I toss it to the end of the deck without opening my eyes. She returns it and dances until I toss it again.

"Hey, Ian."

I jump and blink my eyes until they adjust to the bright sky. I look towards the familiar voice. "Sawyer! You weren't supposed to be here until tonight."

Sawyer is standing at the top of the steps smiling at me. "Great Stevie."

"Oh, shush! Come here." I open the latch and hug him tight. I don't care that he might not want to hug me. I smile when he wraps his arms around me.

"That was the longest two weeks of my life."

"I'm sorry, Sawyer. I should've…"

"No. I was a jerk. I knew you had secrets. I made myself wait until you were able to open up. I was so confused and shocked, I just lost it. I had no right."

"Come inside. I want to get some clothes on so we can talk. Do you have to be anywhere or can you stay for dinner?"

"I'm here as long as you'll have me. But I'd prefer it if you'd stay in the bikini." He winks and gives a click of his tongue.

I run upstairs to change. My heart is racing. I can't believe he's here. He doesn't hate me. "Sawyer, what are you hungry for?" I call down to the living room.

"Spaghetti."

"I should've known." I make my way down the

stairs and look at him.

He's looking up at me with a big smile. "I've missed you so much."

"I want to show you something. I want to share everything with you, Sawyer. I didn't keep things from you because I didn't trust you. I was broken. I guess I still am but I'm working on that." I take his hand and walk over to the fireplace. The box from my mother is sitting on the hearth.

"What's that?"

"This is the box that Mr. Danner brought to me. He said it's from my mother. I haven't even opened it. I wanted to wait until you were here with me."

"Ian, you don't have to do this."

"Please?"

I pull the large pillows from the couch onto the floor while Sawyer starts a fire. I get us iced tea and put CJ outside. When I join Sawyer in front of the fire I notice my hands are shaking. I take a deep breath and cut the tape and then remove the lid.

"Hold on." Sawyer runs into the bathroom and comes back with a roll of toilet paper. "I might need this."

I laugh.

The moment I remove the lid I smell her. I pull out two books. The first is very worn. The spine is cracked and it's obvious it's been read several times. I turn it over to see a big teddy bear in pajamas. The bubbled letters read, "OUR BABY BOY." The pages reveal pictures, dates, weights and hair clippings.

"I had a brother. He died before I was born. As you can see, they loved him a lot." I force the tears from my eyes. "I never knew what he looked like until now. I didn't even know he existed until I overheard them fighting one night right before I ran away."

Sawyer looks at the pages with me. "I can tell he's your brother. You have the same eyes and smile."

"This must be mine." I open the second book. It's pristine. The dates, weights, and few baby pictures are there but it's obvious this book was filled out of obligation, and not love.

There are a few items of baby clothes that belonged to my brother. I pick up a blue shirt with a green monkey holding a banana and hold it to my face, inhaling. My mother must've done the same thing a million times because I smell her perfume deep within the fibers.

Sawyer reaches in and pulls out a faded blue tin can. I know this can. "My parents' beer money." He counts out two hundred dollars and some change. "That's more than I was able to get the night I left. The crackheads would've been pleased."

I take out a manila envelope and draw a breath to prepare myself for its contents. I pull out black and white photos, of me with Jubal. We are laughing.

"I remember that day! Jubal took me into town to get something from the hardware store. I was in a bad mood so he started mocking me. So, I started mocking him. We were cracking up in no time. It was so funny." My heart hurts more than I can explain. I'm so thankful to have these pictures of us.

There are more pictures inside. I drop them in my lap. "She was there! I saw her, Sawyer. I saw her! It was the day I got my hair cut. He yanked me away from a pole. I heard her laughing. But when I looked again, she was gone."

Sawyer sits quietly listening to me explain the items.

I get up and walk to the window. I feel my throat closing on me. I try to make sense of this. She was there. She came to find me. She laughed.

"Are you okay?"

"I need to talk about something other than my parents."

"Okay." Sawyer is talking to me like I might break if he speaks above a whisper.

The only thing I can think of is to tell him about my life with Jubal. "He saved me. He tried to keep me out of his lifestyle but Mikus was such a jerk. I ended up delivering his dope. I'm so sorry." I look up to him for forgiveness.

Sawyer just nods. I continue.

"He had two guys beat the shit out of me. He wanted to teach me a lesson. I figured it out but it was too late. I should've told Jubal right when I saw the backpack in the garage. Maybe he'd…"

"Don't. Don't do that. You can't blame yourself for anything that happened."

I look at the time and realize we have been talking for hours. It's too late for spaghetti. "Do you want to order pizza? I don't think I can boil water at this point."

"Pizza was my second choice." Sawyer kisses the top of my head. "I'll order."

When Sawyer joins me in the living room I'm stoking the fire. I glance at the box like it's a snake that can strike at any second.

"I can't believe she was there. I knew I saw her. But it didn't make sense. Why would she be in Cavern Creek?"

Sawyer pulls me into his arms. He lifts my chin with his fingers and kisses me softly on the lips. "I wish I knew what to say."

"You being here is all I need." I hug him tightly. "Thank you."

I tell Sawyer about the rats. I explain the bite mark and the bruises, and the bruises I had from Mikus. His jaw clenches with every detail until finally the doorbell rings.

Sawyer pays for the pizza. I grab paper plates and napkins. I know I will be unable to eat. We sit back down by the box. I remove a notebook. The edges are frayed and some pages are torn. I lay it in my lap and open it.

"It's poems and gibberish mostly. You can tell by the writing when she was sober compared to the entries when she was lit." I flip from page to page. "Here's the last one."

I knew I'd find you. You're such a fighter.
I didn't know I loved you until you left me.
I stopped drinking and I was good. I was good.
I saw your smile in the picture, but it
was nothing compared to seeing it in person.
Your laughter was music. It plays over and over
in my head.
I can be happy because of you.
I was bad. I drink to forget. It was my fault.
Timmy is gone because of me.
You be free, Vivian. You be free.

"Shit. How did you survive as long as you did?" He pulls me into a tight hug. "You are the strongest person I know. I can see why. You had to be."

I kiss Sawyer. I kiss him with raw emotion. He feels it. He kisses me back. I don't want to talk. I want to feel his skin on mine. I want the world to disappear except for the two of us. He lifts me into his arms and I wrap my legs around him as he carries me upstairs. I pull his shirt off over his head. I don't stop kissing him. He lays me on the bed and our hands continue to remove items of clothing until we are skin to skin. I give myself completely to Sawyer. Nothing to hide. Every part of me is his.

We lie still in each other's arms. It's silent except for our breathing. I focus on matching my breaths to his. "Do you still love me?" I barely whisper.

"I almost forgot." Sawyer reaches for his jeans and pulls a small box from his pocket. "Here's your birthday present."

I open the box and see a beautiful ring. It's a simple gold band with two hearts intertwined. "Sawyer, it's beautiful. Are you sure you trust me with jewelry?"

He is not amused by my joke. "It's a promise ring. You've had my heart from the first time we met. This ring is a promise that nothing will ever change that."

Our breathing slows as we lie together. "I had to save myself," I mumble sleepily.

"What?"

"You asked me how I survived as long as I did. Jubal told me. He said nobody could save me from the rats. He was talking about the nightmares but he was telling me I didn't need anyone to save me. I saved myself."

Chapter Twenty-Eight

"I'll get the dishes. You can go take a bath. My dad sure did like your casserole, huh?"

"Thanks, Babe. And, yes, he did. I'll be sure to make extra next time. I need to run out to the garage before my bath. I scheduled an oil change with Ms. June but can't remember what time."

"I told you she's a great lady. She'll be a loyal customer for life."

"She only likes me because she says I bring her luck. She catches more fish now that we are friends, she says."

I check the calendar on my messy desk and confirm the eight o'clock appointment. I notice the last two boxes that Jim brought over from Jubal's are in the corner. Life has settled over the last several months. The rats have stopped creeping into my sleep. But, so has Jubal. Sawyer has all but moved in. We have dinner with Jim every Sunday and we visit with his parents often. I am happy. I've procrastinated long enough.

I lift the first box onto the grease-stained counter, pulling the tape and lifting the lid. I reach in and retrieve Jubal's wallet, two shirts, his pocket watch and a trinket box with miscellaneous items. I hold one of the shirts to my face, breathing in his scent. I close my eyes and pretend I'm hugging him.

The second box is heavier. Inside, I find riding boots, a helmet, and his leather jacket. When I lift the jacket the air gets trapped in my lungs. I can't scream. I can't exhale or inhale. I just stand there staring at the bright straps of my backpack.

I turn around expecting to see Mikus with his wild

red hair and cocked fists but I'm alone. Of course I'm alone. Mikus is dead. Jubal is dead, because of Mikus. I grab the backpack and throw it into the garbage can. I miss and it hits the floor, sending a small shiny object across the floor. Sawyer's class ring.

I kneel down to pick it up, slowly in case it turns into a snake and strikes. Just as I pull it into my hand, Sawyer comes in.

"Hey."

"Aaaah!" I scream, pulling my fists up ready to fight.

"Whoa! Are you okay? I didn't mean to scare you."

"Oh shit!" I let out a loud laugh. "Come here, look!" I hold out my hand, revealing his ring.

"What the hell?"

"They must've stashed it in the backpack. Jim went to the house to gather some belongings and grabbed it not realizing this is *the backpack*."

Sawyer takes the ring and the backpack, tossing them both in the garbage.

"What the hell?" It's my turn to look at him in shock.

"I don't want any reminder of what happened to you that night."

"But it's your class ring."

"I have you. That's all that matters. Now go take your bath. I want to go to bed." He slaps my butt playfully, raising his brow in a flirtatious hinting manner.

~~~~~~~~

"Come on, Ian! Let's get this show on the road!" Sawyer hollers from the truck.

I lock the door and hand Sawyer the urn before helping CJ into the bed of the truck. I close the tailgate then hop in. "I'm comin'. I'm comin'." I scoot next to him.

"Are you sure you're up to this?"

"For sure. Keeping him in this urn any longer just doesn't seem right. I wish Jim would have come, though."

Sawyer opens my door and carries the urn in one hand and holds my hand in the other. We walk to the *Atticus*, where Patty and Steve are waiting.

When I step aboard I am immediately greeted with a hug from Patty. Steve gives a wave from the wheel.

"Are you okay, Honey?" Patty has both of my arms in her hands and is looking intently into my eyes.

"I am. I really am. I know this is where he wants to be. He talked about this place every day. I can't keep him trapped in this thing any longer. It's time."

"You're not leaving without me, are ya?" Jim is standing on the dock looking a bit pale but determined.

"Jim! Are you serious? You're coming with us? You're coming with us!" I run to hug Jim around the middle and hold his hand as we climb aboard.

"I have something for you." Jim hands me the box under his arm.

I open the long rectangular box to see a beautiful soldered wind chime. It has a square cube with different sized cylinders encircling another smaller cube. There is a bird in flight and a setting sun cut out in the larger cube. The artwork is amazing.

"Jim. It's wonderful."

"It's for your deck. You can hang it on the eave of the house. I took some of the ashes and sealed them in the cube." Jim is holding on to the railing and trying to still his shaking voice.

The rest of us stand there staring at this amazing piece of art. What a beautiful way to give me a piece of both of them. I'm trying not to cry but the tears come anyway. Sawyer takes the chime and I step over to give Jim another long squeeze around his middle.

"How did you ever think of that? I love it. I love you, Jim. Jubal always talked about how special you are. I couldn't agree more."

"You're special to me, too. That's why I'm here with you. Now can we get this over with? I need to get back on solid ground."

"You got it, Jim!" Steve fires up the boat, slowly guiding us out onto the lake.

We drive around until we find a spot and Sawyer drops anchor. The five of us gather at the aft end of the boat and share a moment of silence for Jubal.

"Jubal was my brother. He was funny and smart and brave... and stubborn. He lived a lifestyle that ultimately took his life way too soon. I begged him several times to come stay with me. But he was too proud. I'm glad he didn't listen to me, because had he not brought Ian into my life, I don't know where I'd be. I love you, brother."

Steve and Patty stand there offering support with their presence. Sawyer thanks Jubal for introducing us, and promises to keep me safe and happy. I stare at the waves and wait to be back at home in the comfort of Sawyer's arms and the warmth of my bed. I hold the urn in my arms and stand at the railing. I want to scream up to the heavens to give me back my best friend. I want to say how unfair this is. Instead, I do my best to honor the memory of the greatest man in my life.

"Jubal saved me from a life of hate and showed me love. Pure, unconditional love. He saw me at my worst and loved me even more. He was my friend, my brother, my father, my protector, my nurse and my teacher. I will miss him every day." I remove the lid from the urn and turn it over, letting Jubal's ashes flow into the deep blue water below. "You be free, Jubal. You be free."

The End

www.tracijostotts.com

Evernight Teen ®

www.evernightteen.com

33366098R00150

Made in the USA
San Bernardino, CA
01 May 2016